P9-CKT-355

MARVEL
BLACK PANTHER
SPELLBOUND

MARVEL

BLACK PANTHER

SPELLBOUND

RONALD L. SMITH

LOS ANGELES • NEW YORK

First Edition, September 2021
10 9 8 7 6 5 4 3 2 1
FAC-021131-21225
Printed in the United States of America

This book is set in Adobe Caslon Pro, Century Gothic/Monotype;
The Hand/S&C Type
Designed by Catalina Castro

Library of Congress Cataloging-in-Publication Number: 2021936225
ISBN 978-1-368-07124-6

Reinforced binding

For Chadwick Boseman.
Rest easy, my king.

MARVEL

BLACK PANTHER

SPELLBOUND

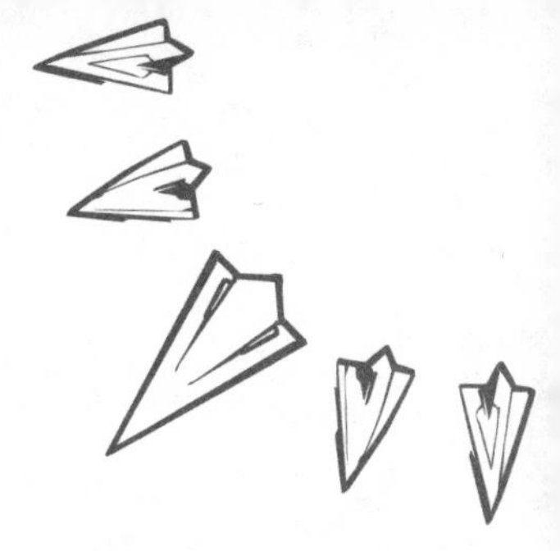

PROLOGUE

The words CLUB FEAR blinked in bloodred neon above the door's entrance.

A stone gargoyle, or some nightmarish creature, perched above it as if surveying its prey.

The stranger, who wore a clean white suit, handmade Italian shoes, and a feathered fedora hat, tapped his walking stick against the door three times. He waited patiently as the spine-rattling thump of heavy bass pulsed from inside.

The solid iron door opened with a groan.

A woman with short red hair and black lipstick stood before him.

"Hello," the stranger said, his eyes hidden by the brim of his hat.

The woman snapped her gum and gave him the once-over. "Yeah?" she asked, not too kindly.

The stranger grinned, and it was a wide grin that seemed to take up his whole face.

"I'm here to see a friend," he said. "His name is Nightmare."

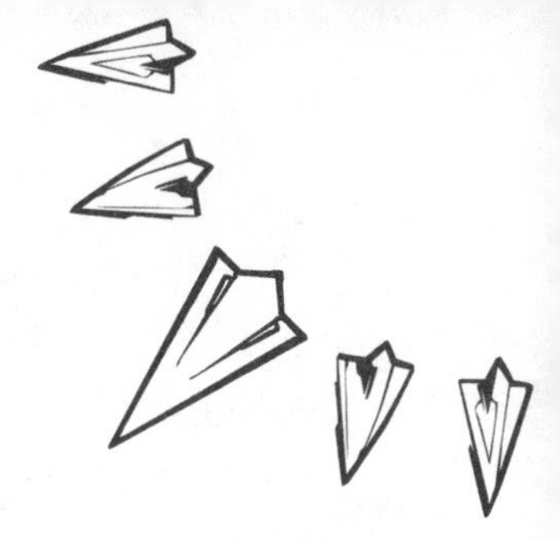

CHAPTER ONE

T'Challa rested his head against the cool glass of the plane's window. He was exhausted.

The flight to Alabama was a grueling sixteen hours, and the last leg of the journey was quickly coming to an end.

The flight attendant, a very tall man with a Southern accent, came through the first-class cabin. "More orange juice, sir?"

T'Challa shook himself awake. "No," he said, rubbing his eyes. "Um, no thank you."

"Very well, sir. We will be landing shortly."

Finally, T'Challa thought.

Even though he was the Prince of Wakanda, a technologically advanced nation hidden from prying eyes on the continent of Africa, he had to settle for a first-class seat on a regular flight—although the hot towels, slippers, and salted cashews were an unexpected treat. Of course, he could have begged his father, T'Chaka, the ruling Black Panther and King of Wakanda, to hire a private jet for the trip. *But then,* T'Challa thought, *where would we have landed?* They couldn't just fly into an ordinary airport. The jet would attract too much attention. Air traffic control would probably think it was a UFO and shoot it down.

Unfortunately, his seatmate, a businessman from a place called Dover, Delaware, tried to engage T'Challa in conversation several times:

"Where in Africa did you say you were from again?"

"Have you ever seen a rhino?"

"What kind of business is your family in?"

Americans sure do ask a lot of personal questions, T'Challa thought.

The only answer he gave, after much persistence, was that the family business was "mining."

A deafening screech jolted T'Challa fully awake. He peered through the window. A flight crew in orange vests swarmed the tarmac, waving their batons. T'Challa released a satisfying sigh. He had pestered his father for weeks to allow him to visit his friends Zeke and Sheila in America. Sheila was spending the summer in Alabama with her grandmother, and Zeke had come in a few days before T'Challa was scheduled to arrive. They had planned it out for weeks through video calls.

Finally, after much back-and-forth, and his father's insistence on T'Challa being careful, the King of Wakanda had allowed T'Challa three weeks' vacation. T'Challa was ecstatic. He couldn't wait to see his friends again.

And now he was here.

He wondered, not for the first time, what surprises the trip would hold.

Outside the International Arrivals gate, T'Challa was met by a wave of sweltering heat—not the dry and pleasant heat of Wakanda, but a stifling, humid heat that made the collar of his shirt stick to the back of his neck.

Footsteps sounded behind him.

He spun around quickly, his defense training kicking in.

A girl with tiny freckles and curly hair stood in front of him. She smiled, revealing straight white teeth.

"Welcome to Beaumont, Alabama," she said.

T'Challa exhaled a sigh of relief. "Sheila!" he said, giving her an awkward hug. Her hair smelled like strawberry shampoo.

"I can't believe you're here," his friend Zeke added, pushing his glasses up on his nose. "I mean, all the way from Wakanda!"

Zeke raised his hand for a high five, and T'Challa returned it.

Zeke was skinny, with close-cropped hair, chunky glasses, and a quick wit T'Challa had seen on several occasions.

"Is that the only bag you brought?" Sheila asked, looking at the glossy black leather shoulder bag he carried.

"Uh, yeah," T'Challa replied. "I didn't bring a lot, and I didn't want to check it."

Sheila fanned herself with a hand and put on an exaggerated Southern accent. "Well, it's so hot here, all you'll need is shorts and a T-shirt, anyway."

Zeke waved her off. "She's been talking like that since I got here."

T'Challa chuckled. The only Southern accents he'd ever heard were from old American TV shows he had watched in Wakanda. "So when did you get here?" he asked Sheila.

"About a week ago," Sheila replied. "I haven't been here in years! The last time was with my parents, and I was like five or six."

"What about you, Zeke?" T'Challa asked.

"Three days ago. I've been researching various food groups." He licked his lips.

Sheila poked a sideways thumb in Zeke's direction. "All he's been doing is eating."

"I'm a growing boy," Zeke said, patting his flat stomach. "Plus, there's a whole lot of food I have to try out!"

T'Challa chuckled again. He'd heard how good Southern cooking was, and he couldn't wait to try some.

Zeke eyed T'Challa's bag with curiosity. "So . . . what'd you bring? Some secret high-tech gadgets? The suit? Please tell me you brought the suit."

T'Challa suppressed a groan.

Last year, on his first trip to America, Zeke and Sheila had found out exactly who T'Challa really was. His father had sent him to Chicago due to a looming threat in Wakanda. Once in the Windy City with his friend M'Baku, they were enrolled at South Side Middle School with fake names. His father didn't want any of his enemies getting word that his son was in America.

He soon became fast friends with Zeke and Sheila, and together, they stopped an evil force that had put the whole school and the world itself in danger. It didn't take long for his friends to discover that he was more than an ordinary exchange student from Kenya, which was his cover. When the threat became so serious that T'Challa had to wear the panther suit his father had given him for protection, Zeke flipped out and wouldn't stop talking about it. It seemed that he was still obsessed.

"Yes, Zeke, I brought the suit," T'Challa confessed. "My father insisted. But he did say to use caution. He doesn't want me getting involved in some kind of dangerous adventure like last time."

Zeke raised a mischievous eyebrow. "You never know, though, right?"

T'Challa shot Zeke a cautious smile.

"Speaking of which," Sheila put in, "how exactly did you convince your father to let you come to America again?"

"It took some pestering," T'Challa replied. "But I finally wore him down."

T'Challa thought back to the moment. At first his father was totally against the idea, but when T'Challa reminded him of how he had handled an unexpected threat on his last trip, and the fact that he was now a year older and wiser, the King of Wakanda nodded thoughtfully and folded his hands together in front of him. It also helped that Queen Ramonda was on T'Challa's side. "T'Challa needs to see more of the outside world," she had said. "The best time to do it is now, when he's young."

After that, his father finally relented.

"Remember who you are," he demanded of T'Challa. "You are a representative of your nation. Use the wisdom and judgment you have been taught. Do *not* let me down."

T'Challa's father had spoken quietly, but the strength behind the words was clear. There was no other way to interpret it:

Do not get into trouble.

"C'mon," Sheila said, pulling T'Challa away. "Mr. Perkins is waiting."

"Mr. Perkins?" T'Challa asked.

"He's like a handyman," Sheila replied. "He does a lot of stuff for my gramma, like cutting grass and fixing stuff. He's waiting for us in the parking lot."

Mr. Perkins, an older Black man with graying hair, didn't speak much but played gospel songs on the car radio. T'Challa hadn't heard anything like it before, but some of the melodies reminded him of Wakandan folk songs back home. He closed his eyes and let the music wash over him, which almost sent him into sleep several times.

After a short drive, Mr. Perkins dropped them off in front of a quaint yellow house with a nice green lawn and giant magnolia trees on either side.

"Thanks, Mr. Perkins," Sheila said. "We really appreciate it."

"Tell Miss Rose I'll be by next week to get rid of that tree stump out back, okay?"

"Sure thing," Sheila replied. "Thanks again."

T'Challa gave Mr. Perkins a smile and a nod, then made his way out of the car.

"Get ready for a wet gramma kiss," Sheila warned T'Challa.

When T'Challa and his friends stepped inside, he was immediately met by an aroma that made his mouth water. He wasn't sure what it was, but he couldn't wait to find out. The living room was large and comfortable-looking, with a big sofa, several wingback chairs, and a large dining area with a massive china cabinet. Pictures of family members were framed on the walls, and fresh flowers sat above a fancy fireplace. A bookshelf took up one wall. T'Challa smiled. Sheila was a big reader and, judging by the numerous books on display, her grandmother was, too. *Must run in the family,* he thought.

"Something smells good," Zeke said as he sniffed the air.

At that moment, a woman appeared from the back of the house. She had short, tightly woven braids and wore a dress printed with bold geometric patterns of green and yellow, which reminded T'Challa of the colorful clothing people wore back home.

"You must be T'Challa," she said, approaching.

T'Challa gulped at the mention of his name, but then realized he didn't need to keep it a secret. She didn't know where he was really from, of course, only that he was a friend of Zeke and Sheila's—one they had met in Chicago as an "exchange student."

Before he knew it, Sheila's grandmother hugged him and planted a kiss on his cheek. "Nice to meet you, T'Challa," she said, breaking the embrace. "You can call me Miss Rose."

"Nice to meet you, too, Miss Rose."

There was a moment of silence. T'Challa stuck his hands in his pockets, not knowing what else to do with them.

"Well," Miss Rose finally said, stepping back with hands on hips. "Who's hungry?"

T'Challa had attended a lot of feasts in Wakanda, but Miss Rose's table was a sight to behold. Zeke pointed everything out. "We got catfish, corn muffins, short ribs, baked mac and cheese, fried okra, boiled peanuts, hush puppies, kale, succotash, red beans and rice, and sweet tea."

"And some Wow Burgers," Sheila added. "They're made from plants." She was a vegetarian but was considering becoming a pescatarian after trying baked salmon.

"Yuck," Zeke complained. "Who wants fake meat?"

"It's healthier," Sheila shot back.

Zeke shook his head and reached for another piece of fish.

T'Challa watched them go back and forth like this for a few minutes. He grinned. This was what they were always like, he remembered. They'd argue, joke, and tease each other for hours, but deep down, they were the best of friends and would do anything for each other if push came to shove. They had both proved that on T'Challa's last trip to America.

"This all looks delicious," T'Challa said, digging into a piece of hot fried fish. The flaky, succulent meat melted in his mouth. He smiled and savored the taste. The food in Wakanda was very good but also a little too healthy for T'Challa's liking—lots of green, leafy plants and lean meats. Any chance he could get to try out new flavors would not be passed up. When he and his friend M'Baku had first come to Chicago the year before, they ate everything in the hotel mini-fridge, and M'Baku got sick from too much chocolate.

Zeke devoured the food like he hadn't eaten in weeks.

Miss Rose looked at him for a long moment. "Child," she said, leaning back in her chair and crossing her arms. "I don't know where you put it all." She shook her head. "Skinny as a beanpole."

"It all goes to my brain," Zeke replied, mouth full.

"Well, you better eat more," Sheila snapped, "because there's a whole bunch of empty space in there."

Even T'Challa had to laugh at that, and he did without hesitation. Zeke mumbled a retort, but Sheila had already won the round.

T'Challa let out a breath and sat back in his chair. He was glad to be here. His time in Wakanda was always full of responsibilities, like meeting with his father's advisors and attending weekly briefings on Wakanda's latest concerns. He also had to oversee a group of gifted students in Wakanda's Academy for Young Leaders, boys and girls who would one day run the government. He did get a little overwhelmed now and then. After all, he had just turned thirteen and still enjoyed Wakanda's lush forests and crystal-clear rivers. He loved tending to the old and disabled animals in the sanctuary, feeding giraffes and rhinos who responded to his soft words and gentle touch. But his father never forgot to remind him of his place and duty in their powerful nation.

You will lead one day, he would say, his voice deep and full of strength. *That is our destiny.*

"So what do y'all have planned for the summer?" Miss Rose asked, bringing T'Challa back to the moment. "Vacation doesn't last forever, you know."

T'Challa's ears perked up at her Southern twang—it was the same tone Sheila had tried to imitate, but this was the real deal.

Sheila reached in her jeans pocket and took out her phone. "Well, I've got it all right here."

"She's a planner," Zeke said.

Sheila scrolled through her phone. "Tomorrow it's the Alabama State Fair. Then I was thinking about a canoe trip on the Tuscaloosa River, and then there's the botanical—"

"Is this just one day," Zeke cut in, "or over the whole summer?"

"Let's start with the state fair tomorrow," Sheila replied, ignoring Zeke's snarky attitude, "and then we'll go from there."

"Sounds like a plan," Miss Rose said. She turned to T'Challa. "What about you, young man? What are you looking forward to?"

T'Challa thought on that a moment. He hoped he could do as much as possible on the trip, but the only thing they had really planned out beforehand was arriving in Alabama around the same time. "Well," he said, searching for a good answer. "It's just fun to see someplace different." He shrugged. "I don't know. I guess I'm up for anything!"

Miss Rose cocked her head. "Sheila said you're from Kenya? So what's that like? I'd love to see the motherland one day."

Zeke and Sheila glanced at T'Challa, wondering what he would say. He didn't want to lie to this nice lady, but he thought he should keep any mention of Wakanda to himself. Most Americans were under the impression that Wakanda was a poor country in need of global aid, but that was all a facade, as Zeke and Sheila knew very well. T'Challa thought it would be easier to just say he was from Kenya, rather than make up stories about how poor Wakanda was. That seemed more of a lie than saying he was from Kenya, to his thinking. He shifted in his chair and scratched his head. "Well," he said. "It's always hot there, like here."

Miss Rose chuckled. "Tell me something I *don't* know."

T'Challa swallowed hard. "There are all kinds of animals. Lots of, um, things to do."

Zeke snorted.

"T'Challa's family is *very* wealthy," Sheila said, which made T'Challa stiffen. "His father is very high up in the government."

T'Challa shot Sheila a look, and Zeke stifled a laugh. *Come to think of it, though,* T'Challa realized, *she isn't lying.*

"Oh, really?" Miss Rose said, seemingly impressed.

"Well, that's very exciting. Guess some of us are just born lucky, huh?"

"Um, yeah," T'Challa said quietly. "I guess so."

"You should see T'Challa wrestle," Zeke said. "Last year, he pinned our old gym teacher, Mr. Blevins, in like thirty seconds flat! It was fast, like . . . *cat* reflexes."

T'Challa gulped.

"Can't say I'm a fan of wrestling," Miss Rose put in. "Why do boys always want to fight?"

"And *that* is the eternal question," Sheila said.

T'Challa sat through this whole episode, trying to keep a smile. His friends were really giving him a good ribbing. It was great to see them again, he realized. He had truly missed them, even if they were putting him on the spot.

"Oof," Zeke said, pushing his plate away and settling back. "I'm stuffed."

T'Challa breathed easier, relieved that the joking was finally at an end.

Zeke's eyes roamed over the remaining food on the table. "Um, what's for dessert?"

Dessert was a choice of peach cobbler or pecan pie, topped with Blue Bell ice cream, one of the South's tastiest treats. T'Challa chose the peach cobbler and ate every bite until he felt his stomach was about to burst.

Afterward, Sheila led T'Challa and Zeke to their room.

It was a small space with bunk beds and a shaggy orange carpet that looked a hundred years old. Zeke had already claimed the top bunk. The room had been vacant since Sheila's two uncles—Miss Rose's sons—moved out long ago. Faded posters of old soul bands were on the walls, along with a beanbag chair, a lava lamp, and a few abandoned toys heaped in an open footlocker.

"Well," Zeke said, stretching his arms behind his head as he lay in the top bunk, "what do you think of Alabama so far?"

But the only response from the Prince of Wakanda was loud snoring coming from the bunk below.

CHAPTER TWO

T'Challa slept peacefully that first night. As soon as his head hit the pillow, he was out like a light, although he woke up with a crick in his neck from sleeping at a weird angle.

After a meal of hot buttermilk biscuits, scrambled eggs, fried potatoes, bacon, and something called grits—which T'Challa had never tried before but enjoyed with salt and a little butter—the trio set out.

Miss Rose's house was not too far from the county line, and they took a bus to the fairgrounds of the state fair. T'Challa peered through the window as they rolled along the bumpy streets. They passed acres of farmland, where cows and horses grazed in green fields. Tractors and farm equipment seemed to be in front of every yard. Red barns loomed in the distance. It was a pleasant scene, and it reminded him a little of Wakanda's agricultural community. The only difference was that in his home country, crops were seeded and irrigated with small hover drones fueled by Vibranium, the nation's most valuable resource—a metal unlike any other, powerful enough to run a city and keep its economy strong. Vibranium was also the chief element in the Black Panther's suit, which provided protection from attacks by absorbing energy and redirecting it back at an opponent. T'Challa had learned just how powerful Vibranium was on his last trip to America, when he defeated an evil creature called the Obayifo, a memory he wanted to put out of his mind forever.

T'Challa reflected on his country's history as he continued to look through the window. Legend said that long ago, thousands of years before our time, a meteor crashed into Wakanda. Bashenga, a warrior shaman of great renown, investigated the wreckage and found a sound-absorbing metal unlike anything he had ever seen. To his dismay, the meteor also gave off a radioactive charge, turning some of the tribespeople into enraged demon spirits. Bashenga fell to his knees and raised his arms to the heavens.

Bast, protect me.

And the panther goddess heard his call.

In a vision, she led him into the forest, where he discovered a mystical plant infused with the strange metal's powerful essence. They called it the heart-shaped herb. Soon after, he destroyed the demons and became the first Black Panther, setting the foundation for generations to come.

Many Wakandans thought the story of Bashenga was only a myth, but T'Challa's father and all the Panther Tribe were true believers, and their rituals and ceremonies were proof of their devotion. T'Challa often wondered about the story, and Bast, especially. Was it all true, or just part of Wakandan mythology?

That same mythology was a constant part of T'Challa's daily life in Wakanda. Growing up, he had heard tales of magic and sorcery—Wakandan legends that explained their history and place in the world. The Ancestral Plane, where people communicated with their dead loved ones, was a reality, along with other seemingly supernatural people, places, and things. *Would Zeke and Sheila believe some of the tales I could tell them?* he wondered.

The bus turned into a massive parking lot full of cars. T'Challa saw hundreds of people headed toward an entrance adorned with banners and colorful flags, snapping in the summer breeze.

"Here we are," Zeke said as they all got off the bus.

T'Challa took in the scene. A giant wheel in the sky slowly turned in a circle above them.

"Are those . . . people up there?"

"Yup," Sheila answered. "The Ferris wheel is my favorite ride of all."

T'Challa blinked. Future Black Panther he might be, but his head still spun at the thought of being so high up in the air.

"What do you want to do first?" Sheila asked the both of them.

"Corn dogs!" Zeke shouted a little too loudly. Sheila closed her eyes and opened them again, as if exhausted.

"What's . . . a corn dog?" T'Challa asked.

"A monstrosity," Sheila replied.

Zeke smirked. "C'mon, T. Don't listen to her. A corn dog is the ultimate Southern cuisine."

"Ha!" Sheila threw her head back and laughed. "I'm sure some highly respected Southern chefs would disagree."

A few minutes later, T'Challa found himself standing in a long line in front of the corn dog vendor. When it was finally his turn, the man behind the counter handed him something skewered on a skinny wooden stick. T'Challa looked at it curiously. "What . . . is it, exactly?"

"An all-beef hot dog coated in batter and deep-fried," Zeke said, a wolfish gleam in his eyes.

"Heart attack on a stick," Sheila added.

T'Challa took a bite. He chewed thoughtfully and then nodded slowly.

"Well?" Zeke said. "Isn't that the best thing you've ever tasted?"

T'Challa swallowed. "Pretty good. Tastes like chicken."

Zeke turned to Sheila and smiled, as if proven right somehow. Sheila just shook her head in dismay.

The sun was blazing as they took in the sights. T'Challa was amazed at the frenzy of activity around every corner. Kids in little cars crashed into one another in a circular arena of sorts. Others got spun around in a cylinder while pinned against the wall. Screaming children dangled arms and legs from spinning machines. Vendors sold everything from a treat called cotton candy to deep-fried cookies. T'Challa felt like he had just landed on some kind of alien planet.

"Step right up!" a man in blue overalls shouted as T'Challa passed him. "Try your strength on the High Striker! How 'bout you, muscles? Wanna give it a try? You're not a wimp, are you?"

For a minute, T'Challa didn't know who the man was talking to. "Me?" he said, pointing to himself.

"Yeah, you, genius," the man shot back.

"Go ahead, T," Zeke said, giving the man a sharp look. "Show him how it's done."

The man was standing in front of a metal tower about twenty feet tall. At the bottom, a small black disc rested on a pad with a spring-loaded metal square next to it. The idea was to swing the mallet and come down hard on the square, which would send the disc all the way up to the top, where it would ring a bell.

"Just fifty cents a swing," the man challenged him.

T'Challa didn't like him. His eyes were narrow and black, like a shark's.

T'Challa patted his pockets. He groaned inside. He had forgotten to exchange money at the airport. Money was something he didn't think about often because he never carried it. Some Wakandans used cash, but most transactions were done through computers and personal data devices, like Kimoyo Cards. Sometimes, though, when T'Challa was out and about back home, one of his bodyguards actually carried real money for him. He knew how privileged he was, and sometimes he hated it.

"Uh, I don't have any change," he said, a little embarrassed.

"Ha!" Zeke laughed. "One of the richest people in Wak—"

Sheila nudged Zeke with her elbow.

"Oww!" Zeke cried, but then his eyes widened. "Oops," he whispered.

"Here you go," Sheila said, handing T'Challa a fistful of coins.

T'Challa gave the man a few coins and picked up the mallet. He tested the weight of it with a few practice swings.

"C'mon, pretty boy," the man said. "We don't got all day. I've got other paying customers."

T'Challa looked left, then right. There were no other customers. He swallowed a reply. The man sure was rude.

"Show him how it's done, T'Challa," Zeke encouraged him.

"T'Challa?" the man scoffed. "What kind of name is that?"

T'Challa ignored him and lifted the mallet over his shoulder. "One," he counted. "Two . . . three!"

He came down hard on the square with all his might.

The disc flew up. T'Challa waited for the bell to ding, but it didn't happen. Instead, the disc hit a small green square that read WIMP and then plummeted back down to land on the pad with a soft plop.

The man burst out laughing. "Aw, isn't that sad? I bet your girlfriend can do better than that!"

Sheila gave the man a look that would melt ice. T'Challa was a little embarrassed, but he wasn't going to let a goon like this get the best of him. He prepared for another try and rested the mallet on his shoulder.

"Let me give it a go," Sheila said, right before he swung.

"Gladly," T'Challa replied. He was tired of this dumb display of brute power, anyway. He handed the mallet to Sheila.

"C'mon, Sheila," Zeke encouraged her. "Show this guy who's boss."

Sheila smiled and stood close to the pad with her feet planted wide apart, like a golfer readying her swing. She looked up the length of the tower and then back down. She mumbled to herself as if she was calculating something in her head, and then took a few halfway practice swings. Finally, she swung down hard, right in the center of the metal square.

The disc flew up the tower.

They all peered up, waiting . . .

DING!

"You did it!" T'Challa and Zeke shouted at the same time. Zeke threw up a hand for a high five, and Sheila returned it.

Sheila took an exaggerated bow. The man smirked again. "Beginner's luck," he chided her. He studied Sheila for a moment and then waved his hand toward the counter behind him, full of teddy bears, fluffy rabbits, and pink unicorns. "What do you want for a prize?"

Sheila looked at the gaudy display of cheap toys. "Nothing," she replied.

"Nothing?" the man snapped. "I thought all you girls liked stuffed animals."

"Sorry, mister," she said, handing him the mallet. "I don't subscribe to gender norms."

The man screwed up his face, trying to figure out if he'd been insulted or not.

"Burn," Zeke said quietly.

"C'mon, guys," Sheila said. "Let's go get some caramel apples . . . wash this sour taste out of our mouths."

"Yeah," Zeke said. "Let's leave this . . . rampallian to himself."

"Rampallian?" the man asked. "What's a rampallian?"

"Read a book," Zeke said as the trio walked away.

"That was cool," T'Challa said. "So how did you do it? I swung that mallet as hard as I could!"

"Exactly," Sheila said with a wry smile, "which is what most men would do. It's not about brute strength, T'Challa. It's about technique. The trajectory of the mallet paired with the gravitational force of the swing is the real key."

"Ah," T'Challa said, still a little confused. He looked at Zeke and shrugged his shoulders. He remembered that Sheila was a wiz at science and technology. Last year, when they had the incident at the school in Chicago, Sheila had hacked into a password-encrypted website in the Wakandan database. And that was just one of her skills.

After incorrectly guessing the weight of a prize pig, seeing their distorted reflections in a fun-house mirror, and buying candy apples—which T'Challa didn't care for; too sticky—they decided they'd had enough of the fair.

"Wait," Zeke said, pointing. "Look over there."

T'Challa followed Zeke's finger. Under a massive red-and-white-striped tent, a man was walking across a tightrope.

"Let's check it out," Sheila encouraged them. "I love acrobats!"

T'Challa felt dead on his feet. He realized he must be having jet lag, but he didn't want to spoil his friends' fun, so he went along with them.

They made their way over but not before stopping at a

concession stand where Zeke bought something called fried dough. T'Challa was beginning to think everything in the South was fried. He tried a piece and soon realized he was covered in white powder, which Zeke found exceedingly funny.

They bustled their way through the crowd. A banner strung across the stage proclaimed:

BOB THE ACROBAT! TIGHTROPE WALKER EXTRAORDINAIRE!

The acrobat walked gently along the rope, long arms held out to either side for balance, testing each step with his weight.

"Amazing," Sheila whispered.

The man stood as still as a statue for one moment. He blew out a breath, then launched himself headfirst in a somersault to touch down once again. The crowd went wild.

T'Challa took a closer look at the man. He was Black and very tall and skinny, with a short stripe of hair running along his head. He wore red-and-gold leggings and a shirt with no sleeves, revealing lean and wiry arms. A black pendant in the shape of a circle hung tightly around his neck.

"Now," the man said, still balanced on the rope, "I will perform a death-defying maneuver, one that only the bravest acrobat would dare attempt."

T'Challa's ears twitched. The man had an accent. West African, he surmised.

An assistant handed the man a black scarf, which he reached down and took, then tied around his head, covering his eyes. The crowd murmured in anticipation. The acrobat stood with his arms at his sides. He put his right foot in front of him and then bent backward at an impossible angle.

"Must be double-jointed," Zeke whispered.

The acrobat took a deep breath, then flung his body into a backflip.

There was a collective gasp.

Time seemed to slow down in that moment, and T'Challa watched with his breath caught in his throat. Seconds seemed to last for minutes until the acrobat landed on his feet again, as nimbly as a cat. He whipped off the blindfold and held out his arms in a grand gesture. The audience once again applauded wildly. The acrobat peered out over the adoring crowd as if looking for someone in particular. Finally, his eyes found T'Challa's. He held T'Challa's gaze for a long moment, and then the strangest thing happened. He gave T'Challa a wide, almost malevolent grin.

Sheila clapped her hands furiously. "Now that was pretty cool!"

"Not bad," Zeke said.

But T'Challa felt differently.

Because there was something about the man that gave him the creeps.

CHAPTER THREE

T'Challa stretched his long legs out in front of him and leaned back in the lawn chair. He placed his hands behind his head. Miss Rose's backyard was a pleasant oasis. The sun beat down in golden rays, warming his face. Birds danced and chirped in the magnolia trees. He had been waiting for summer all year long, and now the duties and responsibilities in Wakanda seemed a million miles away. *Finally,* he thought. *I don't have to do anything, except have fun.*

It felt good to be back in America again, he realized, far from the demands of his father. The King of Wakanda was a hard man who ruled through strength and, sometimes, intimidation, and was not one to wear his emotions on his sleeve.

Will I be like that, too, T'Challa wondered, *when it is my time to rule?*

He knew the day would come in a few short years. His father had won the throne at an early age. Maybe he would expect his son to do the same. *Will I be ready? Can I fill my father's shoes?*

Thoughts of his father gave way to his stepmother, Ramonda. She was the Queen of Wakanda, and while others quaked at her strength, T'Challa found her to be a calming presence and could talk to her about anything, often seeking her counsel before speaking to his father. T'Challa felt she could see things more clearly than the king, and her words were always taken to heart. She spoke softly, but T'Challa sometimes thought it was a ploy to gain one's confidence. Someone once said that Queen Ramonda could slip a knife between your ribs and you wouldn't know until it was too late.

T'Challa's birth mother, N'Yami, died from a rare illness shortly after he was born. He had no memory of her, only holograms and stories from his father. He wished he had known her, and often sought her out in his dreams and prayers to Bast.

But still, he loved Ramonda dearly, as she was the only mother he had ever known.

T'Challa snapped out of his inner thoughts as Zeke came out of the house with two glasses of fresh lemonade. He took the cool, sweating glass in his hand and raised it to his lips. He didn't know which was better, sweet tea or lemonade—and figured he should try several more glasses of each before he made his final judgment.

"So what are we doing today?" T'Challa asked.

Sheila, seated next to T'Challa, looked up from the book she was reading. "Well," she said, "before you got here, all Zeke talked about was finding some real Southern barbecue."

"I did some research before I came," Zeke said. "There's a place called Hatcher's Bar-B-Q that looks really good."

T'Challa patted his stomach. "Well," he said, "I *am* on vacation."

Zeke smiled.

"Where is it?" T'Challa asked.

"It's all the way over in Selma," Sheila replied. "The bus would take forever. Gramma said she'd take us."

"Sounds good to me," Zeke said.

T'Challa remembered that Selma was a historic little town that had seen its fair share of protest and change during the civil rights era. Ramonda had told him that Selma was instrumental in giving Black Americans the right to vote and was now held up as a testament to what could happen when people truly worked together for the good of the country. He once again thought of the disparities between

Wakanda and America. It was something he just couldn't dismiss.

A short time later, they were on their way in Miss Rose's silver Audi A4 sedan.

"Nice!" Zeke exclaimed, settling into the back seat.

"I might be a grandma," Miss Rose boasted, shifting the car into third gear, "but that doesn't mean I have to drive like an old lady!"

T'Challa was surprised, to say the least. Miss Rose drove like a pro and handled the potholes and cracks in the road with ease. When Sheila had told him that they'd be staying with her grandmother, he was a little apprehensive. He had expected her to be a lot older, like grandmothers he had seen in American TV shows and movies. In reality, she was far from that stereotype. Of course, in Wakanda, respecting one's elders was ingrained into the culture. No one would ever think of disrespecting an elder or dismissing them because of their age. They were beacons of history, the storytellers and keepers of tales and legends, and T'Challa listened to every lesson they shared and always heeded their advice.

A few minutes later, the car pulled into a gravel parking lot filled with other cars. A red-and-white sign above the door proclaimed: BEST BARBECUE IN ALABAMA.

T'Challa's nostrils flared the moment he stepped inside. He had never smelled anything so delicious in his life.

He couldn't quite put his finger on exactly what the scent reminded him of, but in the end, he decided it smelled like comfort.

A handwritten menu was posted high on the wall behind the counter and was full of enticing dishes: barbecued beef, pulled pork sandwiches, catfish lunches, mac and cheese, string beans, and all manner of combinations. T'Challa thought Zeke's eyes would pop out of his head.

After everyone had ordered, they found a table and began to dive in. T'Challa had a pulled pork sandwich that was so stuffed with meat, it was falling out of the bun. Zeke went against his first wish and got the smothered pork chops instead of barbecue, as did Miss Rose. Sheila, being a vegetarian, looked at the menu and decided on baked mac and cheese, Southern kale, and hot buttered biscuits.

"Well," Miss Rose said, looking at the feast laid out before them. "This is what I call a real Southern barbecue joint."

T'Challa took another bite of his sandwich. The taste was sweet and tangy and hot all at the same time. He agreed with Miss Rose, but his mouth was too full to speak. Zeke and Sheila moaned with pleasure as they both devoured their meals. They ended with chocolate pound cake, which T'Challa decided right there on the spot was the most decadent thing he had ever tasted.

A short time later, they all sat back and exhaled hearty sighs.

"Worth the trip?" Sheila asked Zeke.

Zeke closed his eyes and shook his head in a gesture of appreciation. "Best. In. The. World."

T'Challa agreed. He looked at his empty plate and thought of Themba, his physical trainer back in Wakanda, who had told him he had to keep up his daily workout if he wanted to become the next Black Panther.

Always time for that, T'Challa thought, and reached for the last slice of pound cake.

CHAPTER FOUR

T'Challa's head bobbed up and down as he slept on the car ride home. He was wiped out—full from the food and tired from jet lag. He only awoke when Zeke slammed the door and got out of the car. T'Challa immediately fell asleep again once he flopped onto the bottom bunk.

Sometime during the night, he had a strange dream. He heard a voice behind a dark veil that could not be pierced. He couldn't make out the whispered words, but he felt as if they were being directed at him, and him alone. The voice was calm and quiet, yet forceful at the same time.

T'Challa awoke and remained motionless in bed, trying to gather his thoughts and recall more of the dream. Vague pictures floated in his mind's eye, but none sharp enough to define. He shook the dream away as he got up and prepared for another hot day in Alabama.

T'Challa and his friends spent the better part of the morning lounging in the backyard and soaking up the sun. He still felt full from last night's barbecue feast. He stretched and inhaled the rosy fragrance of fresh plants and flowers coming from Miss Rose's hanging baskets.

Sheila had pointed them out: "Begonias, moonflower, climbing roses, and Carolina jessamine."

T'Challa loved gardens and taking walks in nature, breathing in the fresh air. Back home, one of his favorite places to relax was a salt marsh surrounded by wild reeds. It was one of the few places he could truly be alone, without a bodyguard following his every move.

A bead on T'Challa's bracelet pulsed red.

Father, he thought. *I never told him I arrived safely.*

For a moment, he didn't know what to do and covered the glowing bead with his hand, but then he realized Zeke and Sheila had seen his Kimoyo Bracelet before.

He got up and walked farther into the backyard and stood under the shade of a magnolia tree, his back to his friends. He tapped the bead. A small screen appeared and hung in midair. Much to his surprise it wasn't T'Chaka, the King of Wakanda. Instead, a young girl peered out at him, a silky coil of braids atop her head.

"Shuri?" he said.

"Hey, big bro," his sister replied. "How's America?"

T'Challa shouldn't have been surprised at Shuri's communication. When he visited America the year before, she was angry he had never called her. Now she was doing it first.

Shuri peered around the holographic image, as if looking for something in particular.

"What are you doing?" T'Challa asked.

"I want to see them," she replied. "Your corny friends. Zeke and Sheila."

T'Challa turned his head to glance at his friends. Zeke's face was buried in a book, and Sheila was sitting in a yoga position, eyes closed. T'Challa turned back around. "Uh, they're busy right now. I'll have to introduce you later."

Shuri smirked. "Promise?"

"I promise," T'Challa said.

Shuri let out a breath. "Father said I could use your hover drone since you're not here."

"What?" T'Challa said, aghast.

A hover drone was a small vehicle powered by maglev technology that was popular among teenagers in Wakanda. T'Challa couldn't imagine his father letting his young daughter drive one unsupervised.

"Well," Shuri said, as if reading her older brother's thoughts, "I *do* have to ride with Uncle S'Yan, but he let me take the wheel a few times. I had an idea to make it go faster. I already have the plans drawn up."

T'Challa couldn't help but smile. Shuri was certain to

make breakthroughs in science and technology before she even earned a driver's license.

"Good," T'Challa said. "Just be careful, sis."

"I will." Shuri paused and lowered her voice. "Listen. See if you can bring me any old American tech. Like their cell phones and stuff. I like taking them apart to see how they run."

T'Challa chuckled. "I'll try, Shuri. I gotta go. Tell Father I arrived safely, okay?"

Shuri nodded. "I will, but make sure you call back so I can talk to your friends?"

"You bet," T'Challa replied.

Shuri stuck out her tongue, and the image flashed out.

T'Challa shook his head.

He headed back over and flopped onto the lawn chair. His skin felt like it immediately stuck to the material.

Zeke closed the book he was reading. "So, I was thinking we could go see the Iron Man," he said.

T'Challa did a double take.

"Not *that* Iron Man," Zeke clarified.

Sheila roused herself from her sitting yoga position. "He means Vulcan."

"Vulcan?" T'Challa repeated, still at a loss. He had no idea what his friends were talking about.

"He's the Roman god of fire and the forge," Zeke said.

"Oh," T'Challa said, recalling his Greek and Roman mythology. "*That* Vulcan."

"We gotta check it out," Zeke said excitedly, pushing his glasses up on his nose. "This guidebook says it's the biggest cast-iron statue in the world. His head weighs eleven thousand pounds!"

"Slightly less than yours," Sheila added.

"I'm game," T'Challa said. "Let's check it out."

There were bus rides all around Alabama for sightseeing and history tours, and it was only a short walk from Miss Rose's house to get to one. After buying bottled water at the convenience store next to the station—Zeke bought several sweet treats called MoonPies—T'Challa and his friends made their way onto the bus. There were lots of families and tourists on board, but the trio found seats in the same row. Fortunately, the bus had the AC turned on high, so it was a relief from the intense heat outside.

"Want one?" Zeke asked, handing T'Challa a MoonPie. He was trying out so many new foods, his head was spinning.

"Nah," T'Challa said. "I probably shouldn't."

"C'mon," Zeke pressured him. "You did say you're on vacation, right?"

T'Challa relented and unwrapped the package. It looked like a little round pie with chocolate on the top and bottom.

"It's got marshmallow inside," Zeke said.

"What's marshmallow?" T'Challa asked.

Zeke opened his mouth in exaggerated surprise. "Oh, my god, Sheila! The boy has never had marshmallow!"

T'Challa blinked.

"Guess he's never had s'mores, either," Sheila said. "Sad."

"What's a s'more?" T'Challa asked.

"Maybe we'll take you camping and you'll find out," Zeke replied mysteriously.

"S'more," T'Challa whispered, befuddled.

"Try the MoonPie," Zeke encouraged him. "Go on."

T'Challa took a cautious bite. He chewed for a moment. "Mmm," he murmured. "This is really good!"

"You guys keep eating like this, you're gonna get sick," Sheila warned them.

T'Challa finished his and wanted another, but he decided against it. Sheila might have a good point, he realized. Instead, he sat back and tried to enjoy the ride, but every time he closed his eyes, Zeke would nudge him and point out the window. The last time he did it, T'Challa was surprised to find that he wanted him to look at a cow. *A cow.* "We have those, too, you know," T'Challa admonished him. "Cows."

After that, Zeke let him get a few minutes' rest.

It didn't take long to get to Birmingham, where Vulcan Park was located. T'Challa remembered that both Birmingham and Selma were at the heart of the civil rights movement in the 1960s. People like Rosa Parks, John Lewis, Martin Luther King, Jr., and other brave souls spent their lives fighting against racism and injustice. That was a long time ago, he realized. What was Wakanda doing while the United States was going through all this? Did his country help, or did they just stand by while the wheel of history turned? He made a mental note to ask his father about it when he returned home.

T'Challa spotted the Vulcan statue before they even got off the bus. "Wow," he said, craning his neck up. "That is awesome."

And indeed it was. It soared at least six hundred feet in the air, T'Challa guessed. The giant figure held what looked like a spear in a massive outstretched hand, with fingers as long as telephone poles. A bearded face peered out over all of Birmingham.

"It says here that it's fifty-six feet high and weighs fifty tons," Sheila read from a plaque when they reached it. "*And* it's the tallest statue besides the Statue of Liberty."

"Cool," Zeke said. "Let's go inside."

After talking to a tour guide, they learned that they could walk up a flight of stairs or take an elevator to the observation deck.

"Stairs," they all said at the same time.

The winding circle of steps made T'Challa's head just a little bit dizzy. They were the only ones inside, and their voices echoed around the empty space. T'Challa wiped sweat from his brow.

"This is a good workout," Sheila said as she climbed the interior stairwell, checking her heart rate on her watch. Zeke huffed and puffed but didn't complain. T'Challa didn't find it difficult at all. He was in peak form from his exercises and training in Wakanda. They reached the top not a moment too soon. Zeke was sweating, and his glasses kept sliding off his nose. A warm breeze caressed T'Challa's face. "Ah," he said, taking in the air.

A circular platform ringed the statue's pedestal so people could walk around the sculpture and take it all in. T'Challa and his friends hurried to the railing and looked out over the city. T'Challa noticed a few families as well as a man with a small boy who shouted and clapped as his father held him up on his shoulders.

"Amazing," Zeke said, out of breath.

The view was spectacular. The whole city could be seen from the Vulcan's perch on the famous Red Mountain. Zeke and Sheila took pictures with their phones while T'Challa continued to admire the view. He had to admit it was pretty cool.

T'Challa turned at the sound of raised voices.

"What the—?" Sheila started.

A strangely dressed man had arrived on the observation deck.

"Is that . . . ?" Sheila said.

"Bob the Acrobat." Zeke finished the sentence.

T'Challa looked at the man closely. That was definitely him—the same man from the state fair. There was something about him that T'Challa found unsettling. When he was younger, Ramonda had given him a children's book called *Alice's Adventures in Wonderland*, where a character called the Cheshire Cat boasted a grin that was way too wide. That's who T'Challa thought of when he looked at the acrobat.

"What's he doing here?" Sheila whispered. "Some kind of performance?"

They didn't wait long to find out.

Very quickly, and without looking at anyone in particular, the man reached over his left shoulder and pulled a long coil of rope from his backpack. The tourists watched in anticipation, their voices suddenly quiet. T'Challa didn't see any kind of security on the platform at all.

"Ladies and gentlemen," Bob said, and his voice was strong and somewhat deep, carrying past the observation deck to the blue sky beyond. "Can I have your attention?"

T'Challa had no doubt the man was from West Africa now. He heard it in the pronunciation of the word *attention*.

"Consider yourselves very lucky," he continued, "for this will be a special day you will always remember. You have the best seats in the house."

Cell phones came out, and people started recording.

T'Challa looked on curiously. Bob caught his eye. T'Challa could have sworn that the man winked, as if they were in on some kind of private joke. *He's definitely following me,* T'Challa thought. *How else could we be here at the exact same time?*

No, another voice in his head countered. *You're just being paranoid.*

The acrobat uncoiled the rope and made a loop, then

twirled it above his head like an American cowboy and threw it high in the air, toward the spear that Vulcan held. T'Challa was surprised to see that the rope caught the spear on the very first try. Bob smiled and then gave a short tug, testing that it was fastened. And then, to T'Challa's and everyone else's amazement, he began to pull himself up the statue, planting his feet out from his body like a mountain climber.

"He's gonna go all the way to the top!" Zeke shouted.

A burst of static from a walkie-talkie blasted in T'Challa's ear. A burly man in a uniform appeared from the stairway, huffing and puffing. "Hey, you!" he called out. "Come down at once!"

But Bob paid him no mind and continued his ascent.

T'Challa wondered why the acrobat was doing this. He was reminded of a giant spider as the man climbed. As he became smaller and smaller, T'Challa shaded his eyes with his hand, trying to block the sun and keep the man in sight. People were murmuring and pointing, excited and fearful at the same time.

"What in the world is that man doing?" one said.

"He's crazy," added another. "Someone's going to get hurt!"

And as they continued to watch, Bob the Acrobat reached the peak of Vulcan's head. He took a deep breath . . . and then . . . launched himself into a handstand.

But what happened next was the grand finale.

As he stood on his hands, Bob's legs swayed forward, and he let himself fall.

A woman screamed.

"Somebody call nine-one-one!" a man shouted.

"My god!" Sheila cried, reaching for her phone.

People rushed to the railing.

T'Challa was stunned, but as he was about to run for help, he saw, along with everyone else, two wings, like those a paraglider would use, snap out from Bob's body and lift him up on great gusts of air.

Zeke pointed to the sky. "Look."

"Unbelievable," Sheila whispered as Bob became smaller and smaller.

T'Challa squinted. Something was floating on the air. At first he thought it was a flock of birds, but then he realized they were sheets of paper drifting down from the sky like giant snowflakes.

Another security guard appeared and started asking questions.

"Bob must've dropped those from his backpack," Sheila suggested.

"Maybe it's just a big promotion for his show at the state fair," Zeke added.

"Seems like a long way to go for that," T'Challa said. "A long, long way."

Whether by chance or some unknown extrasensory

warning, T'Challa turned away from the spectacle to see a young boy, four or five years old, with one leg straddled over the guardrail. T'Challa's heart jumped in his chest.

"No!" a man cried out as he pointed at the child.

The bars between the beams were less than a foot apart, too narrow for someone to slide through, but this boy had climbed up the bars and was about to go over.

A bolt of adrenaline raced through T'Challa's body. He had to act, and fast.

T'Challa flew forward like an arrow released from a taut bow. The boy dropped a toy Vulcan statue in his effort to climb over, which fell to the depths below. T'Challa had only seconds—milliseconds.

He had to be careful. He didn't want to startle the child, but he had to be quick.

With catlike reflexes, he grabbed the boy around his middle and scooped him up, then pulled him free of the bars to safety. T'Challa exhaled a relieved breath as he set him down.

"Matthew!" a man shouted.

A young man with sandy-brown hair rushed over and dropped to his knees, sending the two sodas he was carrying crashing to the ground. He hugged his child fiercely. "I wanted to see if I could fly, Daddy!" the boy said, not realizing the danger he had narrowly escaped. "Like the man with wings!"

The boy's father, crying now, squeezed his child tight, and finally noticed T'Challa standing next to him. "Thank you, friend. Thank you." His face was a map of alarm and fright. "I only stepped away for a second. I—" He stopped short, at a loss for words.

"You're welcome, sir," T'Challa told him.

Zeke and Sheila stood with mouths agape, stunned by T'Challa's quick thinking and reflexes.

"Black Panther to the rescue," Zeke whispered.

"Quick thinking," Sheila said. "That was nuts."

"Which part?" Zeke asked. "That kid or Bob the Acrobat?"

"Both," Sheila replied.

"I had to do something," T'Challa said. "There was no time to lose."

They made their way toward the exit. T'Challa was still a little shaken by the child's close call. He exhaled a heavy breath.

"Look," Sheila said, stooping to pick up something from the ground.

T'Challa and Zeke looked over her shoulder. It was a flyer printed with the silhouette of a human form with outstretched arms and legs within a circle.

T'Challa studied the image. "This looks like the Vitruvian Man."

"You're right," Zeke said. "That's what Bob must've dropped from his backpack."

T'Challa saw that other people were also picking up the flyers, as if Bob had deliberately left them behind in order to be discovered.

"What does Leonardo da Vinci have to do with Bob?" Sheila asked.

The security guard was now directing people away from the monument. The police had arrived and were asking questions.

But T'Challa's thoughts were elsewhere.

Who was Bob the Acrobat, and why did he suddenly seem to be everywhere T'Challa was?

CHAPTER FIVE

The next morning, news of Bob the Acrobat's flying adventure was in the local papers and all over the internet.

ACROBAT SCALES VULCAN STATUE, JUMPS

"Well, if he wanted to get attention, he sure did," Sheila said.

The trio sat around the kitchen table while eating fresh cinnamon rolls for breakfast. Miss Rose was at church, her refuge every Sunday morning, Sheila had told them. T'Challa was interested in going as well, but Sheila said he would never make it out if he did. The sermons were long, she warned him, and people in the South went to church on Saturday and twice on Sundays. T'Challa decided he'd have to experience it on his next trip, if the day ever came.

T'Challa thought back to Bob's flying stunt. "I think this guy is up to something, but I don't know what. I know he's from somewhere in Africa. I could hear his accent when we were at the fair."

"Aren't you being a little paranoid?" Sheila suggested.

T'Challa balked. Was he being suspicious for no good reason? The man *had* grinned at him, though. That wasn't his imagination.

"Hmm," Zeke murmured. "You were saying something about his accent. Not Wakandan, though, right? You'd know if he was from Wakanda."

"He doesn't know *everybody* in Wakanda, Zeke," Sheila said, and then, turning to T'Challa: "Do you?"

"No," T'Challa replied. "There's something familiar about him, though."

"Bob," Zeke whispered. "Who's called Bob?"

"Uh, lots of people," Sheila said.

"Right," Zeke shot back. "But his name doesn't match his appearance. It's gotta be a fake name of some sort. He's probably named Sidewinder or, I don't know—the Mad Acrobat! You know, something more dramatic. We gotta find out who he really is!"

Sheila stared at Zeke like he had three heads. "This isn't a movie, Zeke. He hasn't really done anything to cause alarm." She paused. "Well, other than jumping from a giant statue."

"So how does this Vitruvian Man flyer fit in?" Zeke asked. "What does it have to do with him?"

T'Challa had been wondering the same thing. Sheila took out her phone and did a quick search.

"Listen," Sheila said. "'Leonardo da Vinci's Vitruvian Man is known as the divine connection between the human soul and the universe. It's mankind existing in heaven and nature at once, and in perfect harmony.'"

"That's what I was gonna say," Zeke said flatly.

There was a moment of silence.

T'Challa thought about what Sheila had just read. *A divine connection between the human soul and the universe.* It was a beautiful thought, he realized, and he wanted to look into it further.

"Well," Zeke said, finishing the last of his cinnamon roll. "I'm tired of talking about Bob, whoever he is. We need to do something fun."

T'Challa heard the front door open and then footsteps.

"Who's that?" Zeke asked.

Sheila stood up. She glanced at the clock. "It's only ten o' clock. Gramma's still at church."

T'Challa traded a wary glance with Sheila. "Gramma?" Sheila called.

"It's me, honey," a voice called, and Miss Rose stepped into the kitchen.

T'Challa exhaled a sigh of relief.

"Gave me a fright," Sheila said, sitting back down. "I thought you were at church."

"The pastor wasn't feeling well. You remember Mr. McGuire?"

"Oh, yeah," Sheila said. "He runs that bookstore, too, right? The one Mom used to take me to when we visited?"

Miss Rose sat down. "That's him, honey. He gave his sermon and then excused himself. Said he was coming down with something."

"Hope he's all right," Sheila said.

Miss Rose reached for a cinnamon roll. "I'm sure he'll be fine. One of those summer colds, probably." She studied them all for a moment. "What are you kids up to today?"

"Not sure," Zeke said.

"Oh, really?" Miss Rose replied. "You mean you're not looking for someplace new to eat?"

T'Challa chuckled.

"Whatever we do," Zeke said lightheartedly, "there will be food involved."

Miss Rose shook her head. "Child eats more than a bear getting ready for hibernation."

Sheila put her head down and laughed. T'Challa tried to hide his amusement but thought he would crack up at any moment. Miss Rose just had a way about her.

"You got any ideas on what to do today, Gramma?" Sheila asked once she had gained her composure.

Miss Rose took a bite of her roll, set it down, and chewed thoughtfully. She nodded to herself. "Well, back when your uncles were still here, there was only one place they would go on weekends."

"Where?" Zeke asked.

"The Arcadium," Miss Rose replied.

"R-*who*?" Zeke asked.

"It's an arcade," Miss Rose said. "You know? *Pac Man* and *Space Invaders*? This was before all those games y'all kids play on computers."

"Oh!" Zeke said, his eyes lighting up. "My dad told me about those games."

"The Arcadium is one of the last few video arcades in the country," Miss Rose explained.

"Sounds like fun," Sheila said.

"I'm game," Zeke added. And then: "See what I did there? *Game?*"

Sheila rolled her eyes.

A short bus ride later, T'Challa found himself standing in front of a machine with blinking lights and loud, cartoonish music accented by bangs, whistles, and crashes. The noise was overwhelming and bounced around the whole place. Several kids and adults hunched over the old-school machines and grimaced and muttered as they furiously smashed buttons.

"Keep going!" Zeke encouraged T'Challa between bites of greasy nachos. "Get 'em!"

T'Challa bent over the machine, his reflexes lightning fast. The game was called *Space Invaders*, and as he fired at the little aliens floating down from the top of the screen, Zeke gave a play-by-play commentary.

Meanwhile, Sheila was challenging another girl at a game called *Bubble Bobble*, where you had to capture enemies inside of bubbles.

T'Challa fired furiously as the last few space invaders rained lasers down on him.

"One left!" Zeke shouted. "Go right! No, left!"

T'Challa destroyed the final enemy of the round and raised his arms in triumph.

"New high score!" Zeke congratulated him as lights flashed and alarms blared from the machine.

T'Challa turned away from the noise, his eyes wide with adrenaline.

"What?" Zeke asked.

"I wanna go again!" T'Challa half shouted.

Two hours later, after T'Challa and his friends had played pretty much every game in the arcade and spent all of Sheila's and Zeke's money, Sheila suggested they best be getting back.

"One more game," Zeke said. "I never did challenge you at *Frogger*."

"You sure?" Sheila replied.

Zeke's determined game face needed no answer.

Twenty minutes later, Zeke was still saying he could have won if the machine had been placed on a more level floor.

"Excuses, excuses," Sheila teased. "I beat you fair and square."

"I demand a rematch," Zeke countered.

Sheila smirked. "Maybe next year, sucker."

Zeke shook his head in disbelief as they all headed for the exit.

T'Challa stepped aside as a man in a green suit with a shock of black hair almost walked right into him.

"Excuse me, friend," the man said.

"Sure," T'Challa replied as they passed each other.

They made their way out the door. For some reason, T'Challa was compelled to turn around. There was something about the man he found . . . odd. Was it the green suit? Or his spiky black hair, which looked like it had been plugged into an electrical outlet?

As T'Challa turned around, he found the man had done so as well. It was then that the man made a strange gesture. He bent his head sideways, then clasped his hands together as if praying and laid them to the side of his head, making the universal gesture for sleep.

"Weird," T'Challa whispered, turning back around quickly before his friends noticed.

"What?" Sheila asked.

"Nothing. Just some strange-looking man."

Zeke and Sheila both turned around, but the man had vanished.

"Beaumont's not the biggest city," Sheila explained, "but we've got all sorts: goths, hipsters, nerds. You name it."

"Right," T'Challa said.

But he still felt unsettled.

He didn't think the Man in the Green Suit fit any of those descriptions.

CHAPTER SIX

T'Challa lay in bed. The glow of the lava lamp provided a calming effect—a myriad of slowly swirling colors of red, blue, and green. He thought about Bob the Acrobat and the Man in the Green Suit. The last time he had come to America, he discovered he was being followed. That time, it was Nick Fury, sent by his father to keep an eye on him.

Was he being followed again?

T'Challa turned over and punched his pillow, making a soft spot to rest his head. *Sheila's right. I'm just being paranoid.* He turned off the lamp and fell asleep to the sound of Zeke's light snoring.

▲▲▲

The next day dawned bright and sunny, like every other since T'Challa had arrived. The jet lag was finally wearing off, and he stretched and yawned in bed. "About time," he said aloud.

After a quick breakfast, the group set off on a little sightseeing tour in and around Beaumont. It was a small, quaint town with a rich history. There was an old train depot that had been turned into a museum, a few shops where artists sold their paintings and sculptures, and several small businesses that sold everything from hand-woven baskets to African-inspired clothing. T'Challa was glad to see a connection to his homeland in this little town, thousands of miles from the world he knew. He bought a small wooden carving of a panther to give to Shuri.

T'Challa thought back to when he left Wakanda, and how Shuri was jealous that he was allowed to visit America. "Your time will come," their father had told her. "Maybe one day you and your brother can go together."

Shuri had smiled reluctantly and wished T'Challa a safe trip. She was like that, T'Challa knew: kind, smart, and determined. More often than not, one could find her in Wakanda's science labs, soaking up information like a sponge. She had the run of the place, being the princess, and her quest for knowledge was insatiable. T'Challa knew her future would be bright.

As they continued to explore Beaumont, T'Challa saw, as he had in Chicago, a few areas that were run-down and in need of renovation. Boarded-up buildings and abandoned storefronts dotted the streets. He thought it strange that America had so much wealth, yet some of its citizens couldn't escape poverty. He made a promise to himself to help one day, if he could.

He thought once again of Wakanda's wealth and prosperity. *What can we do to make our neighboring nations better? When I rise to the throne, my reign will be one of open borders, sharing Wakanda's wealth and technology.*

But, another voice in his head chimed in, *how will you do that? Wakanda's power lies in its secrecy. Would you give that away for a humanitarian cause?*

"Not everywhere gets the same treatment as the nice historic part," Sheila said.

T'Challa snapped out of his thoughts.

"Lots of businesses have closed up," Sheila went on. "Gramma said that mining used to be the town's main industry, but the last mine closed decades ago. That's where my granddaddy used to work, before he died."

T'Challa thought of the Great Mound in Wakanda, where Vibranium was mined deep underneath the slopes of Mount Bashenga. When he was a kid, his father would buckle young T'Challa into the Royal Talon Fighter, the king's personal aircraft, and take him to see how it was done. Hover drones floated around the mound, their lasers pinpointing locations where rich veins of the unearthly metal could be found. Subterranean mine carts powered by maglev technology raced to the depths to return with a huge glittering bounty.

T'Challa knew that Sheila's grandfather would have marveled at the technology. "Too late now," he whispered.

"What's that?" Sheila questioned.

"Nothing," T'Challa said.

As they made their way to the bus stop, T'Challa saw a group of three or four people headed their way. They took up the whole sidewalk and were taping flyers to telephone poles and lampposts.

"Here you go," one man said as they passed. "Big rally coming up." He handed T'Challa a flyer and kept walking. T'Challa took it as the group proceeded down the street.

"What's it say?" Sheila asked.

They huddled alongside him. It was a flyer printed on red paper—one they had seen before.

"Vitruvian Man again," Zeke said.

But on this one, there was a message:

RALLY FOR JUSTICE

JUNE 9

8 PM ON THE TOWN GREEN

MEET THE GOOD DOCTOR, BOB

"I guess the flyer from Vulcan Park was just the tease, as they say in advertising," Sheila said.

“Who’s the Good Doctor?” Zeke asked. “What kind of name is that?”

“I don’t know,” Sheila said. “But that rally is tomorrow.”

T’Challa was really intrigued now. What was this Bob up to? He had looked directly at T’Challa on two occasions, and that was more than a coincidence.

“We should check it out,” Zeke suggested.

“Okay,” Sheila said. “But I really don’t think anything weird’s going on.”

T’Challa nodded, but he wasn’t quite sure that Sheila was right.

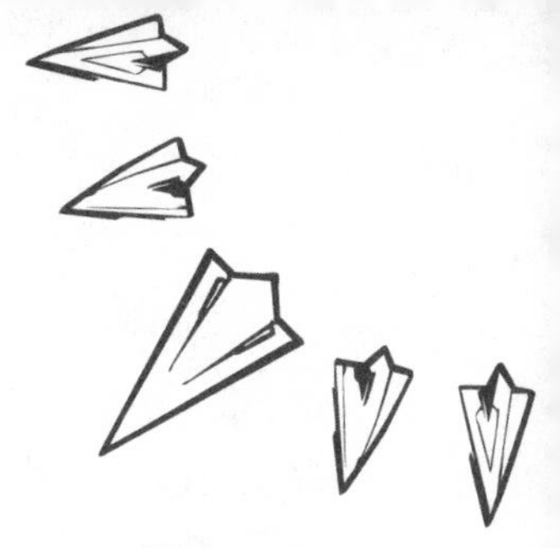

CHAPTER SEVEN

T'Challa sat down to a bowl of hot Southern chili. As hot as it was in the South, people still ate hot food even on the warmest of days. Food was food, Miss Rose had said, and it was eaten in the South no matter the temperature.

"So what do you kids have planned for the evening?" Miss Rose asked, setting down a plate of corn bread.

Sheila slid her spoon into her bowl. She had chili as well, but without the meat. "There's some kind of rally going on at the Town Green. We were thinking about checking it out."

"Oh, really?" Miss Rose said. "What kind of rally?"

Zeke placed a dollop of sour cream on his chili. "It's some sort of social-justice thing. I think."

Miss Rose smiled. "Still fighting for change. We did that, too, back in the day. Sometimes it seems like we're still fighting the same battles."

A thoughtful gleam sparked in her eye. "When your mama was just a baby, I'd carry her to protests. We thought we could change the world."

"You did change the world, Gramma," Sheila told her. "What you did back then was amazing! Mom told me that you and Granddaddy used to go into stores and restaurants and demand to be served. Now that's brave."

"Thank you, child," Miss Rose said. She cocked her head. "And to think we did it all without the internet."

Zeke looked up from his bowl. "I still don't understand how that worked. How did you talk to each other if you couldn't text?"

Miss Rose closed her eyes and opened them again. T'Challa had seen Sheila do the same thing several times the past few days. "Zeke," Miss Rose said. "There were these things called *telephones*."

"Oh, that's right," Zeke said, feigning surprise. "You actually had to memorize phone numbers." He went back to his food. "Weird."

"You wanna come, Gramma?" Sheila asked. "To the rally?"

"You kids go on and fight the power yourselves," Miss Rose replied. "I did my time already."

"We will, Gramma," Sheila said with a smile. "We will."

The Town Green was a historic, parklike area that was home to city hall, the old state house, a library, and a few more government buildings. A nicely manicured green space with tall elms and magnolias provided plenty of shade for people to sit or gather for events. T'Challa and crew walked from Miss Rose's, and he was sweating by the time they got there.

"Well," Sheila said. "Here we are."

"Right," T'Challa replied. "Now we can find out more about this Good Doctor character."

"If that's even his real name," Zeke put in.

There was a moment of silence. The smell of grilled meat wafted on the air.

Zeke's nostrils flared. "I'm hungry."

"When are you not?" Sheila said.

Zeke followed the smell of barbecue and left T'Challa and Sheila standing alone. T'Challa took in the sights. The Town Green was full of people, mostly older men and women, who stood in small groups eating or talking. A makeshift stage was set up with a wooden podium in the center and speakers on either side. A gospel song floated out over the crowd. T'Challa felt something stir deep inside him when he heard the music. It was sad and uplifting at the same time. A combination of emotions ran through him as he stood there. In his mind's eye, he saw generations of Black men and women working the land and being denied the most basic of human principles. He found it troubling, to say the least.

T'Challa came out of his reverie to find Zeke standing beside him, eating a hot dog. A spot of yellow mustard dripped from his chin. He handed T'Challa a cold lemonade. "Thanks," T'Challa said, taking the drink. He raised the straw to his lips and took a long sip. Somewhere nearby, the distinct sound of drumming rang in his ears. "Where's that coming from?" he asked. "The drums."

"Over there," Sheila said, pointing to a group of people gathered around a large statue of a man astride a horse, his sword thrust out in front of him. Someone had set up speakers, and a bass-heavy track boomed throughout the area. T'Challa saw that a number of the people held hand-painted signs.

"What's that all about?" he asked.

"A protest," Sheila replied. "I heard they're here all the time. They want that statue to come down. It's been on the Town Green for years. I think—"

"Is that Miss Sheila I see?" a man's voice called out.

T'Challa turned to see an older white man with a snowy beard approaching. He was reminded of a character he once read about called Santa Claus.

Sheila's eyes lit up.

"Mr. McGuire?"

"The one and only," the man replied.

Sheila reached up and gave him a small hug. "How did you even recognize me?"

"How could I forget Miss Rose's granddaughter?" Mr. McGuire said. "She used to bring you into the store when you were little. With you and your mom."

"Oh," Sheila said, turning back to her friends. "Zeke, T'Challa, this is Mr. McGuire. I was six years old the last time I saw him, and I still recognized him!"

Mr. McGuire tugged at his chin. "Gotta be the beard."

"He owns an antique shop with old books and lots of cool stuff," Sheila explained.

The big man offered his hand, and T'Challa shook it. He had a grip like a bear. "Nice to meet you, T'Challa," he said.

"You too," T'Challa replied.

"How are you, Mr. McGuire?" Sheila asked. "Gramma said you weren't feeling too well in church."

Mr. McGuire exhaled a heavy breath. "Much better. Must've been one of those twenty-four-hour bugs."

"Good," Sheila said.

The squeal of a microphone brought their conversation to a halt.

"Looks like they're getting ready to start," Sheila pointed out.

T'Challa turned toward the stage. He did a double take.

A few men and women, who looked like security of some sort, were wearing T-shirts emblazoned with the Vitruvian Man symbol. They stood on either side of the stage, their arms crossed and their expressions blank.

"Strange," T'Challa said under his breath.

Zeke looked as well. "Weird," he whispered.

"Better get a seat," Mr. McGuire said, scooting past them. "Good to meet you all. Say hi to Miss Rose for me, Sheila."

They exchanged good-byes and Sheila, Zeke, and T'Challa took seats in the folding chairs. T'Challa found himself sitting behind a lady with a hat that looked like a giant bird. Fortunately, he was tall enough to see over it.

"Okay," Zeke whispered. "Let's see what this . . . *Bob* is all about."

A crack of thunder jolted the audience to attention. T'Challa looked to the sky. Dark clouds loomed in the distance.

A hush fell over the crowd. The gospel music slowly faded to be replaced by the deep, ominous notes of an organ, which made T'Challa's chair rattle and vibrate. He felt the bass notes ripple along his spine. Ater a moment, a man walked out from the left side of the stage.

Zeke nudged T'Challa.

The man called Bob wore a red suit and a white shirt. *Flamboyant,* T'Challa mused. *A showman.*

A hat—T'Challa thought it was called a fedora—was

cocked on one side of his head. His shoes were black and stylish, with sharp, pointed toes.

Bob walked to the podium, and T'Challa heard his shoes clicking on the stage. He leaned down to the microphone, then raised his arms. "Welcome," he said.

His voice was so deep, T'Challa felt it in his chest. The crowd murmured a greeting in return.

Bob raised himself to his full height. He was even taller than T'Challa remembered. A quick vision of the acrobat leaping from the Vulcan statue flashed through his memories.

Bob looked out at the audience. He didn't speak for a long moment, as if he were waiting for something, but T'Challa didn't know what. "Citizens of Beaumont," he finally began. "I am here today to talk about . . . *power*."

"Amen," someone shouted.

Bob's gaze wandered over the audience until he found who had spoken. "Yes," he said, in an almost mocking tone. *"Amen."*

The crowd was quiet, and T'Challa thought it strange that it was so solemn.

"Power is what drives men and women to do great things," Bob continued.

Several people in the audience nodded in agreement.

"But sometimes"—Bob pulled the microphone from the stand—"power is used to keep people . . . *down*."

"Preach," the woman in front of T'Challa called, then fanned herself with a church fan.

"What's he getting at?" Zeke asked.

"Shh!" Sheila whisper-shouted.

"Take, for example," Bob said, "this great town of yours. Beaumont. You all know who Beaumont was, don't you? You've got a statue in his honor right over there." He pointed a long finger behind the audience. T'Challa turned to see the monument he noticed before, the protestors still gathered around it.

"That's right," Bob said, gesturing to the protestors. "I see you. We need more people like you, willing to take a stand."

Several people in the audience turned and looked at the protestors.

"For those of you who don't know," Bob went on, "that's a monument to General Clifford Beaumont. One of the South's favorite sons. How many years has it stood as a reminder of the Confederacy?"

People shifted in their seats. "Too long!" one of the protestors shouted back.

T'Challa looked on curiously and listened. He had heard about the recent upheavals in the US surrounding the Confederate flag. But this Bob was from Africa. How much did he really know of America's history? Was he using this as a way to rile up the people of Beaumont?

Bob paused and let the moment rest. T'Challa suddenly recalled an American movie he had seen long ago, where a Baptist preacher brought his congregration to a standing ovation with his fiery words. Bob had the exact same mannerisms.

Bob looked out at the crowd. "I'd say it's high time that abomination came down!" he shouted.

The protestors raised their signs higher and gave shouts of support. Bob waited patiently for their cheers to fade. "But your local government does *nothing*," he hissed, stalking across the stage now, a lion hunting prey. "They want it there . . . as a reminder. You know what they say: Stay in your place. Don't cause trouble. . . ."

T'Challa stole a glance at Sheila, who was nodding along.

"But sometimes," Bob went on, "trouble is what it takes to make a *change*. Look at your schools . . . all run-down. The last iron-ore mine closed years ago, and now even crime is on the rise!"

A clap of thunder jolted T'Challa from his seat. The crowd suddenly fell quiet. The storm clouds were moving in closer now, pulsing with jagged lightning strikes.

Bob looked to the sky and then back to his audience. "But today, my friends, the Good Doctor is here to help. Today, I want you to join me in a new movement. A movement that will bring about *change*. A movement I call . . . Rising Souls!"

On cue, a banner unfurled from a raised bar behind Bob, showing the Vitruvian Man and the words RISING SOULS in bold type.

People stood and clapped their hands furiously.

"Rising Souls," Sheila whispered.

"What does that even mean?" Zeke asked.

Bob peered out over the crowd, his head held high, then raised a hand for quiet, which fell immediately. "And *our* first act"—he pointed to the statue again—"will be to take . . . that . . . thing . . . *down*!"

"Yes, sir!" someone shouted.

"Amen!" called another.

The protestors chanted now, banging drums and blowing whistles.

"Matter of fact," Bob said, sticking his neck out like a cobra preparing to strike. "Why are you folks waiting? I say we destroy it . . . *now*!"

To T'Challa's amazement, people rose out of their seats. Bob jumped from the stage and landed gracefully on the ground. He began walking toward the statue. "Uh-oh," Sheila said.

"This could get ugly," Zeke added.

But T'Challa and his friends were swept up in the crowd that had fallen behind Bob.

Before T'Challa knew it, several people from the audience climbed onto the statue's granite pedestal and began to rock it from its base. The protestors cheered and cried out, pouring all their frustrations into this one singular mission.

"Look out!" Sheila cried, pulling Zeke away from the giant tilting horse and rider.

Bob was suddenly on the top of the base, his feet planted firmly apart. "One!" he shouted, and pushed hard on the statue. "Two!" he cried out, and the people joined in. *"Three!"*

The statue of General Clifford Beaumont, the South's favorite son, came down with a tremendous thud, creating a huge impression in the soft earth. People shouted and raised their hands for high fives. Cell phones came out of pockets to capture the moment.

And all the while, Bob stood triumphant, his foot atop the fallen stone general as rain burst from the swollen clouds overhead.

"Bob!" the crowd shouted. "Bob! Bob! Bob!"

"C'mon," T'Challa said. "We better get out of here."

The trio left quickly, with the sound of police sirens wailing in the distance.

CHAPTER EIGHT

"He whipped the crowd up into a frenzy," Zeke exclaimed, his mouth full of lemon pound cake.

"Rising Souls?" Miss Rose said. "Sounds . . . interesting."

They sat around the kitchen table and told Miss Rose everything.

"What do you think about all this, T'Challa?" Miss Rose asked. "You ever have anything like this happen in Kenya? Protests and such?"

T'Challa shifted in his seat. He swallowed. "Well, kind of. There are different political factions trying to gain power. My father always says—"

Sheila's eyes widened.

"What's that?" Miss Rose asked. "What about your father?"

T'Challa's mouth went dry. "Um, my father. Yes. Well, he says that people can be influenced very easily. All you have to do is find someone for them to blame—someone they can lay all their fears and anxiety on."

"Ain't that the truth," Miss Rose said.

"Oh," Sheila said. "Mr. McGuire was there, too."

Miss Rose cocked her head. "Mr. McGuire?"

"He said it must have been some kind of bug," Sheila explained, "but he's feeling better now."

Miss Rose nodded. "Guess he still has that fighting spirit. He *was* on the front lines back in the day."

They sat together in a rare moment of silence. T'Challa eyed the lemon pound cake, but he wasn't hungry. He was thinking of how strange it all was. This man Bob had come out of nowhere and now seemed to be everywhere he and his friends were. It had to mean something.

"Well," Sheila put in, "whoever this man is—Bob, Good Doctor, whatever—what he said was true, about the statue and all that, but it's like he was doing it just to provoke, you know?"

"That statue did need to come down, though," Zeke said. "For real."

"Got that right," Miss Rose said. Sheila nodded in agreement.

T'Challa took in all the conversation quietly. If he

wanted to, he could find out exactly who Bob really was. He had brought some tech with him from Wakanda—even though he didn't tell Zeke and Sheila that—and he could use it to do some research. But, truth be told, he didn't necessarily want to. As he had thought several times before, this was just supposed to be a fun summer getaway.

"Well," Sheila said. "All this drama has me pooped. I'm out."

Sheila rose from the table and stretched, then yawned. T'Challa felt the urge to yawn as well but tried to resist. A few minutes later, though, he couldn't hide his fatigue any longer, and after a "good night" to Miss Rose, he and Zeke followed Sheila.

But not before Zeke snagged another slice of lemon pound cake.

T'Challa rolled over in bed.

He was wiped out. Maybe the jet lag hadn't worn off after all. Then again, it could have been all the food he was eating that was making him sluggish. Tomorrow he would do his daily push-ups, he told himself.

"Hey. You awake?"

Zeke's voice was quiet but loud enough to bring T'Challa out of his thoughts. "Yeah," he said.

Zeke sighed. "I was just thinking about this Bob dude."

"What about him?"

"Rising Souls. What do you think that means? Maybe he's trying to start some kind of cult or something."

T'Challa considered Zeke's comment. He didn't really get the feeling Bob was starting a cult. "What kind of cult?"

Zeke shifted around in the top bunk. "I don't know. A cult of flying acrobats?"

T'Challa laughed and it came out as a snort. He yawned. His eyes were heavy. "I'm tired, Zeke. Let's talk about it tomorrow, okay?"

"Okay," Zeke said, somewhat forlorn. "G'night, T'Challa."

"G'night, Zeke."

T'Challa turned over to lie on his other side. Even though he was dead tired, his mind continued to race. Was Zeke onto something? Was Bob trying to start a cult of some kind? Why was he using the Vitruvian Man as his symbol? And, T'Challa continued to think, what was Bob doing in Alabama in the first place? Was he trying to get the people of Beaumont to put their trust in him, and if so, for what reason?

T'Challa sighed and stared at the lava lamp, which was becoming a nightly ritual. His eyes opened and closed slowly. The colors seemed to give him an inner peace of some sort, as if he were falling into a bright and colorful dreamscape. . . .

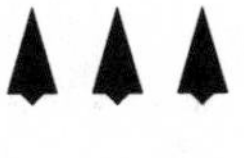

Blackness loomed ahead.

Not the blackness of night, but a more profound darkness. The kind of darkness from which there is no escape, a suffocating emptiness.

The ground was soft under T'Challa's feet. Cool, damp air drifted around him. He didn't know where he was, but in his head, a voice called out—a voice he had never heard before, one that sent a shiver along his bones:

Young Prince. We will meet where the sand runs like blood.

The voice seemed to penetrate his skull, a sharp declaration that was also a warning.

T'Challa paused.

Something ahead of him flashed, just for a moment—a face.

Maniacal laughter suddenly rang in his ears. He whipped his head left, then right, and finally up.

The disembodied face of Bob the Acrobat hovered in the air above him, grinning from ear to ear. He came closer and closer, laughing wildly the whole time, his teeth as broad as white fence posts.

T'Challa woke suddenly, beads of sweat dotting his forehead. For a moment, he thought he was back in Wakanda, until he heard Zeke's constant, steady snoring. He sank back onto the bed. Gray light peeked through the curtain. He looked at the clock: 3:30 a.m. He turned his pillow over and tried to calm his mind.

But he couldn't.

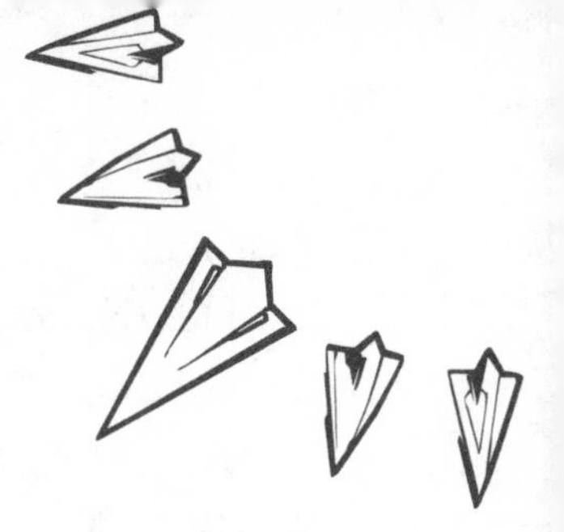

CHAPTER NINE

T'Challa shook himself awake. His head was muddled. He looked at the bedside clock: 9:30 a.m. *How did I sleep so late?*

Slowly, an image of the dream he had last night came back to him: Bob's leering face, grinning at him. And the voice, calling his name. *We will meet where the sand runs like blood.*

Bob isn't really talking to me in a dream, is he? T'Challa wondered. That would make him some kind of supernatural being, and that was something he did not want to consider, not after his last adventure in America.

But still, it had happened.

What does it mean?

He released a heavy sigh, then dressed and headed downstairs.

To his surprise, the kitchen was quiet, even though Sheila, Zeke, and Miss Rose were all around the table. Miss Rose rested her forehead on a closed fist and shook her head. Sheila and Zeke wore glum faces.

"What happened?" T'Challa asked in a soft breath.

Sheila nudged her tablet in front of him, and T'Challa looked at it:

LOCAL PASTOR/ANTIQUE
SHOP OWNER MISSING

Beaumont Police have begun a search for Charles McGuire, the respected and admired pastor and owner of McGuire's Antique Emporium. The store was not vandalized, but police suspect burglary. McGuire was last seen at a rally coordinated by a new organization called Rising Souls, headed by a man who goes by the moniker Bob, the Good Doctor. A small riot broke out after the event where the landmark statue to General Clifford Beaumont was destroyed. Local police are also investigating that disturbance. Anyone with any information on Mr. McGuire's disappearance is urged to call Beaumont Police.

T'Challa finished reading. He looked at Sheila. "This is the man we just met? The one at the rally?"

"Yes," Sheila said. "I can't believe it. We just saw him."

Miss Rose lifted her head. T'Challa saw that her eyes were wet. "Charles is a dear friend and a good man," she said, sniffing. "I've known him twenty-five years! Who in the world would want to harm him?"

"I don't know, Gramma," Sheila consoled her, reaching out for her hand. "The police will find out. I'm sure of it."

"They called it a riot," Zeke complained. "Far from it."

"What do you think they were looking for?" T'Challa asked. "The people who broke in?"

Sheila shrugged. "He has all kinds of valuable stuff in there: old books, coins, stamps, little odds and ends."

"What is this world coming to?" Miss Rose said in an exhausted tone. "Right here in Beaumont!" She shook her head again and studied all three of them with a careful eye. "I want y'all to stay close. Understand me, Sheila?"

"Yes, ma'am," Sheila said contritely.

T'Challa sank down into his chair.

His trip to Alabama was beginning to feel very strange.

The next few days passed uneventfully, and the trio stayed close to home at Miss Rose's insistence. T'Challa thought she was being overly cautious—it was awful what had happened to Mr. McGuire, but that wasn't proof of some kind of mass kidnapping scheme. T'Challa was still troubled by the dream of Bob's face.

Where the sand runs like blood.

What could such an odd message mean?

Today was quiet, and the trio played a game in the backyard called croquet, which T'Challa had never heard of. He wasn't very good at it, but Zeke was and won every round they played.

Afterward, they all sat down and cooled off with lemonade. There was a long moment where they didn't speak at all, as if they were all lost in their own thoughts. Finally, T'Challa broke the ice.

"I had a dream," he said.

"Congratulations," Zeke replied.

Sheila looked up from her tablet. "What kind of dream?"

T'Challa shifted in his chair. He took another swig of lemonade and set the glass down. "Bob was in it. It was his face, staring at me."

"That's not too strange," Zeke said. "I mean, we *have* been talking about him a lot. It must be your subconscious. I was reading this graphic novel about this alien race that feeds on our minds when we sleep. . . ."

"Interesting," Sheila said, which made Zeke sit up and smile.

"There was something else, though," T'Challa said. "Something really weird."

Zeke and Sheila leaned in.

"He said, 'Young Prince. We will meet where the sand runs like blood.'"

No one spoke. A bird landed on the table and quickly fluttered away.

"He said 'Young Prince'?" Zeke asked. "That *is* strange."

"You said his accent sounded familiar," Sheila said. "Are you sure he doesn't know who you are? It just seems really strange that he would say that, even in a dream."

"I know," T'Challa said.

"Where the sand runs like blood," Sheila murmured.

T'Challa frowned. "In my culture, dreams are always omens. They tell us what we need to know, and we take them seriously. Sometimes they're messages from the ancestors, warning us of danger."

"How can Bob speak to you in dreams?" Sheila asked.

"Like I said," Zeke persisted. "The subconscious. I've heard of stuff like this in comics. Bad guys can always invade your dreams."

"This isn't a comic," Sheila scolded him.

"Well," Zeke shot back, "do you have any explanations?"

Sheila looked down at her tablet and started typing. Zeke shared a glance with T'Challa. A minute later, Sheila said, "I don't see any references to where the sand runs like blood. There's something about Normandy and World War Two, but that's about it."

"We'll have to keep searching, then," T'Challa said. "It has to mean something."

"Sounds supernatural," Zeke said softly, as if he didn't really want his friends to hear.

But T'Challa did. And it worried him.

Sheila's face was grim. "Let's hope not," she said.

The water sprinkler suddenly clicked on, startling all of them.

T'Challa inhaled, then looked to Sheila and Zeke.

"We need to look for him," he said.

"Who?" Zeke asked.

"Mr. McGuire," T'Challa answered.

Sheila studied T'Challa.

"Well, he is a friend of your grandmother's, right?" T'Challa pointed out. "And you, too, Sheila."

Sheila remained quiet for a moment. She rapped her knuckles on the table. "T'Challa's right. Gramma's known him forever. We have to at least try."

"It's settled, then," Zeke said, leaning back. "The Black Panther Crew rides again!"

T'Challa released a breath. After everything he had told himself about getting embroiled in another adventure, here he was about to do exactly that. He had no choice, though, he argued with himself. Sure, the police would be looking for Mr. McGuire, but couldn't he and his friends do the same? The more people looking, the better chance of him being found.

T'Challa took another long drink and set down the glass. "So," he said. "Where do we start?"

CHAPTER TEN

"The first thing we need to do is see if we can get into Mr. McGuire's store," T'Challa said.

"The scene of the crime," Zeke added.

The trio had turned the basement of Sheila's grandmother's house into their Base Camp. It was a big room with an old pool table with a damaged felt top, a boiler that belched, shook, and rattled, a tattered sofa, and a ragtag collection of old chairs and side tables.

Zeke had brought his laptop and Sheila, her tablet. Under a faded tapestry on the wall, hidden from prying eyes—namely Miss Rose's—Sheila had printed out pictures from the internet that showed Bob jumping from the Vulcan statue and the crowd toppling the monument. The article describing Mr. McGuire's disappearance was taped to the wall along with the Rising Souls flyer. T'Challa didn't know if they were connected or not, but they had to start somewhere. *And*, since Bob also appeared in his dream, it didn't seem like a leap to think they were linked. T'Challa leaned back in his chair and studied the wall.

"So," he started. "Is there any connection between Mr. McGuire and Bob?"

"Don't think so," Sheila said. "I mean, we saw him at the rally, but that's about it."

T'Challa nodded thoughtfully. "Is there anyone else who works at the store with him?"

"Let me check," Sheila said. She flipped open her tablet and started typing. T'Challa bounced his leg up and down like a piston.

"Well," Sheila said after a minute, "besides a store cat called Fred, there's a girl named Mika who's doing a summer internship. Look. There's a picture of her."

T'Challa and Zeke leaned into the tablet to get a look. Mika had dark skin, short platinum hair, and a small gem in her left nostril. Her eyes were an unusual brilliant green.

"Maybe we can find her," Zeke suggested. "She might know if any strange people came into the store lately."

Sheila shook her head. "I don't want to profile anybody."

"Me either," Zeke said. "I'm just saying we can kind of, like, interview her and see what she knows."

T'Challa pondered this for a moment. He rubbed his chin. "I think you're both right. We don't want to assume anything about anyone, but if we ask her who's been in lately, she might be able to provide some clues."

"Let's get to Mr. McGuire's store, then," Sheila said, closing the top of her tablet, "and see what we can learn."

"Right," Zeke agreed. "Let's do this."

Sheila promised Miss Rose that they weren't going far and that they just needed to get out of the house for a while. She hesitantly gave permission but delivered a stern warning about staying in touch and to let her know if they were going to be late for dinner.

McGuire's Antique Emporium was situated along Beaumont's Antique Row, one of the oldest neighborhoods in town. All along the street, T'Challa saw shops with display windows featuring everything from Persian rugs and refurbished furniture to fancy silverware and old-fashioned globes of the world. People bustled along, taking in the sights. T'Challa made a mental note to come back and shop if he ever got the chance.

After another block, they came to a store with a massive window display of books stacked upon each other. A hand-painted sign of an inkpot and quill above the door read: MCGUIRE'S ANTIQUE EMPORIUM.

Zeke took a picture of the storefront with his phone.

"Here goes," T'Challa said, and they stepped inside.

A chime sounded as he opened the door. It was dark and a little dusty, but still had a homey, pleasant atmosphere and a sort of organized chaos to it. The smell of old books filled the whole space. Murky oil paintings hung on the walls, and tall ladders leaned against bookshelves that rose all the way to the ceiling. Decorative objects filled tables and shelves: old watches, jade elephants, small busts of Greek and Roman figures, sepia-toned photographs, antique perfume bottles, and Fred the cat lounging on a pile of tattered books, ignoring everyone.

T'Challa noticed a young woman behind the counter. Her hair was more silver than it was in the picture. She wore a T-shirt that read THE BOOK WAS BETTER THAN THE MOVIE. Sheila was the first one to approach her. "Hi. You're Mika, right?"

After explaining that she and Miss Rose were friends of Mr. McGuire's, Mika smiled brightly. "Ah, oui!" she said. "Your grand-mère has come in before. She is a lovely woman. Très chic."

Sheila smiled politely. T'Challa noticed Mika's accent. "Êtes-vous française?" he asked.

Mika's green eyes lit up. "Ah, oui! Ma famille est de Saint-Martin."

"Ah, très bien," T'Challa said. "Je suis en vacances d'Afrique."

"Oh," Mika said. "Where in Africa?"

T'Challa swallowed hard. "Uh, Kenya."

"Ah, très jolie," Mika replied.

Sheila and Zeke exchanged glances and raised eyebrows. "Show-off," Zeke whispered. T'Challa was the teacher's pet in French class last summer because he was fluent. The only French verb Zeke could conjugate was *manger*, which meant "to eat."

"We're sorry about Mr. McGuire," Sheila said. "It's terrible."

Mika sighed. "Yes, it is, Sheila. The police came in and looked around and took pictures but said I could keep the store open."

Sheila glanced quickly at T'Challa and took out her phone. She scrolled through her photos before holding it up so Mika could see. "Did you see anybody who looked like this in the past few days?"

Mika leaned in to get a closer look of Bob jumping from the Vulcan statue. "Oui," she said. "I remember him. He came in looking for a book."

T'Challa felt his stomach pitch. *Bob was here.* Sheila shot him a knowing look.

"Book?" Sheila repeated, turning back to Mika. "What book?"

Mika rose from her stool behind the counter and turned around to view a row of books on a shelf, most of them old and almost falling apart. T'Challa saw several cracked spines, and some books that looked as if they would crumble to dust if touched. Mika whispered to herself in French as she searched and then went back to English. "Mr. McGuire kept all of the valuable books behind the counter," she said, "first editions and such." She ran her finger along a row of spines. "Hmm," she murmured.

"What?" T'Challa asked.

"It was right here," Mika said quietly while continuing to look. "It's gone."

T'Challa's stomach flopped again. "What . . . was the book?"

Mika answered but lowered her voice, as if talking to herself. "Monsieur McGuire thought it was valuable, but he didn't know for sure. He found it at a trader's bazaar in Morocco. It was a big book, with . . . how do you say . . . symbols?"

"Yes," T'Challa said. "It had symbols on the cover?"

Mika turned around. "Oui. Little . . . pictures."

Something stirred inside T'Challa. A book with strange symbols on the cover. He had to know more.

"Mr. McGuire didn't want to sell it, you know?" Mika continued. "He said it was a—how is it called—a showpiece?"

"So," T'Challa pressed her. "The title?"

Mika shrugged. "I do not know."

T'Challa felt his hopes fade.

"Un moment," Mika said.

T'Challa, Sheila, and Zeke all shared hopeful glances.

Mika took a sheet of paper from the counter and picked

up a pen. "These . . . symbols," she started as she began to sketch. "They looked like this."

Mika's tongue darted to the corner of her mouth in concentration as she drew. "There," she said after a moment. "Voilà."

She held it up.

T'Challa saw what looked like a broken chain, a crescent moon, and a star.

"These were on the book," Mika said.

"Strange," Zeke whispered.

"Can we keep this?" T'Challa asked.

Mika gave T'Challa an inquisitive glance.

"Just in case we find it," T'Challa said, a little nervously.

Mika shrugged. "It is okay, since you are friends of Monsieur McGuire."

"Thanks," Sheila said.

They exchanged good-byes and headed for the door.

Once outside, Zeke said, "What the heck kind of book could it be?"

"I don't know," T'Challa replied. "But we're going to find out."

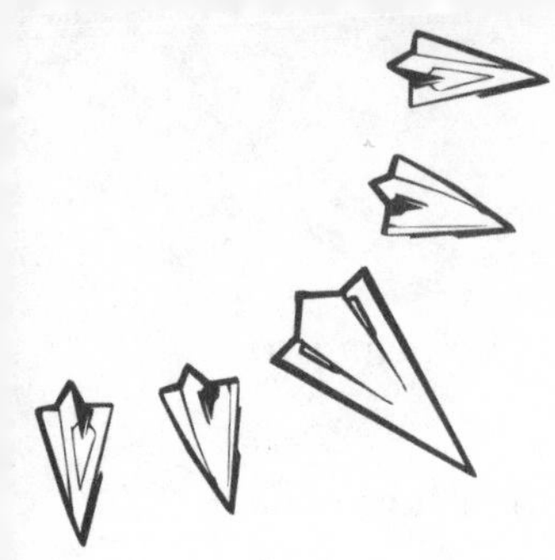

CHAPTER ELEVEN

T'Challa felt out of sorts as they walked back to Miss Rose's. The street was full of dog walkers, joggers, and people distracted by their phones. He had to move out of the way several times to avoid being bowled over.

Something weird was happening. He couldn't put his finger on it yet, but it was a feeling, a feeling he had experienced before—one of menace, just out of reach, directed at him. He had experienced this same premonition when he was in Chicago the year before.

"We have to find out more," Sheila said pointedly. "It's starting to get really weird. Think about it: T'Challa's dream, Bob being in the store, and now a strange missing book?"

"All the ingredients for an adventure," Zeke said.

"Mr. McGuire's missing, Zeke," Sheila said. "This isn't all fun and games, you know."

Zeke wilted a little. "I know," he said defensively.

T'Challa shot him a sympathetic look.

Sheila paused. "I'm sorry, Zeke. I didn't mean to snap. It's just . . . Mr. McGuire is a family friend. Gramma's worried, and so am I."

"It's okay," Zeke said. "I understand. We're gonna do everything we can to find him. Right, T'Challa?"

"Right," T'Challa replied.

After Miss Rose saw that they had all arrived back home safely, the trio headed down to Base Camp. T'Challa withdrew Mika's sheet of paper and smoothed it down on the table. He stared at it for a long time, as if it were some kind of logic puzzle. "A chain, a moon, and a star," he whispered.

Zeke threw a handful of gummy bears into his mouth and typed furiously on his laptop for several minutes. "Hmpf," he said. "Never seen that before."

"What?" Sheila asked.

"I tried every combination of search terms: old book, star, moon, broken chain, Morocco, and nothing comes up. What could these symbols mean? What kind of book doesn't have a name?"

"One that doesn't want to be discovered," Sheila said, her voice dire.

T'Challa continued to stare at Mika's symbols. He knew what he had to do, but he was still hesitant.

"What?" his friends asked at the same time. They knew him well enough to know when something was bothering him or when he was trying to keep a secret.

"Be right back," he said, and darted up the steps, leaving Zeke and Sheila staring at each other, dumbfounded.

He returned a moment later, carrying the black leather bag he had arrived with. He rummaged around inside it and withdrew a silver case, then set it on the table.

"What you got there?" Zeke asked, his voice full of anticipation.

T'Challa didn't answer, but placed his thumb on a small circle in the center of the case. After a moment, the circle began to glow red.

"Wow!" Zeke exclaimed.

The circle slowly went from red to green. T'Challa waited a moment and then pressed the circle. The top slid away like a secret panel to reveal a black-velvet-lined case.

"I need one of those," Zeke said.

Sheila and Zeke took a closer look. Several items were nestled within the case.

"So you *did* bring some tech," Zeke said, his eyes lighting up.

T'Challa picked up a silver cuff about two inches wide. A black screen was embedded in the center.

"That's the cool watch!" Zeke said. "Like the one we got after you left!"

T'Challa smiled and recalled a pleasant memory. When he had returned to Wakanda last year, his father had Nick Fury make a special delivery to Zeke and Sheila. It was a holographic watch, just like T'Challa's, so they could all keep in touch. The only rule was that they couldn't show it off to anyone, which was half the fun of having it, according to Zeke.

"We left ours back in Chicago," Zeke said, his face glum.

"Airport security," Sheila added. "We thought they might get confiscated or something. They'd probably think it was some kind of spy tech."

"Wait a minute," Zeke suddenly said, cocking his head. "How did you get *your* stuff through security?"

T'Challa smiled. "Zeke, my friend, there's some Wakandan tech I can't even tell you about."

Zeke stared, anticipating.

"What does that mean?" Sheila put in, curious now.

"Well," T'Challa said, "I'll give you one clue. It's called cloaking illusion, and that's all I'm gonna say."

Zeke's mouth fell open. "Cloaking? Like invisibility?" He looked to Sheila. "Ah, man! You gotta tell—"

"Maybe one day," T'Challa said, cutting him off, then returned the watch to the case. Zeke looked like a puppy whose treat had just been taken away.

T'Challa reached back in the case and picked up a beaded bracelet.

"Kimoyo Bracelet," Sheila said.

Zeke peered at the Kimoyo Bracelet. It looked like an ordinary string of beads, but it was much more than a fashion accessory. Each bead was branded with a silver glyph, a symbol of its purpose. Citizens of Wakanda received them at birth, where they were equipped with a Prime Bead, which stored their medical records and other vital information. Other beads were used for mobile communication, GEO tracking, and AV screen projections.

T'Challa slipped it on his wrist, alongside the one he had used earlier to contact Shuri.

"Two of them?" Zeke asked.

"One is just for simple holographic communications," T'Challa said.

Sheila turned to Zeke. "Simple . . . holographic . . . communications," she said without emotion. "That's all. No biggie."

Zeke shook his head at the marvel of Wakandan technology.

T'Challa tapped one of the beads. A wispy trail of what looked like white smoke streamed from the bead and then formed into a small screen of warm blue light, which hovered in the air. Zeke stared intently. "What are you gonna do?"

"Well," T'Challa said, "we're going to find out what that book is all about."

Zeke turned to Sheila and smiled, giddy with excitement.

T'Challa waved his wrist over the sheet of paper, which suddenly appeared on the screen, still hanging in the air.

"I'm going to try a deep search of all the databases in the world," T'Challa said, "from VPNs to onion servers to the dark web. There has to be something somewhere."

"Onion servers?" Zeke asked. "What's an onion server? A waiter who brings you onion rings?"

T'Challa managed a laugh. Sheila smiled and turned to her friend. "An onion server is like . . . the skin of an onion. It's an encrypted network. There are layers and layers and layers, and when you peel the last one, you get your result."

"Wow," Zeke said. "You should go on *Jeopardy!* someday."

"I plan on it," Sheila said.

T'Challa twirled a bead on his bracelet.

"I don't understand how your search function works," Sheila said. "Does it use Boolean logic?"

"Boo-what?" Zeke asked. "Wait a minute. First onions and now boo— Whatever. You guys are speaking another language."

Sheila steepled her fingers together. "Boolean logic, or Boolean algebra, was invented in the nineteenth century by a mathematician named George Boole. Basically, it uses three operators—*and*, *or*, and *not*—to determine if values are true or false."

Zeke looked at Sheila. "Oh," he said.

"You understand it better than I do," T'Challa confessed.

"All I know is what the techs in Wakanda told me. Which is pretty much what you just said." He scratched his head. "I guess."

Zeke shrugged his shoulders. "Just do it, then. Um, the *boo* thing."

T'Challa waved his hand over the small screen, which then floated to the wall and expanded to the size of a large monitor.

"So. Freaking. Cool," Zeke said.

T'Challa walked the few short steps and touched the screen with his index finger. There was a whirring sound, and then a pleasant voice asked:

What is your query?

T'Challa looked at Zeke, then Sheila. "Decipher symbols," he said. "Chain, moon, star. Add old book, Morocco, valuable. Utilize Boolean operators."

Mika's drawings suddenly grew larger, with a red border around each one. Below the drawings, the screen morphed into a black circle. A sliver of red appeared along the curved bottom and began to pulse.

"It's searching, right?"

"Correct," T'Challa said. "The technology not only scans for the search term, but anything ever associated with it, and then filters down to the most relevant results."

The circle was now almost completely red. T'Challa waited with nervous energy. A beep sounded, and then the voice replied:

Result. Search terms found. Symbols are associated with an ancient tome known as *The Darkhold*.

"*Darkhold*," T'Challa whispered.

The room suddenly felt colder to T'Challa, and a chill crept across the back of his neck.

The voice continued:

Also known as the Book of Sins. Believed to have been created out of dark matter by Chthon, Archdemon of Chaos, the first demon god.

"No," Sheila whispered. "Oh my god."

T'Challa froze where he stood. Zeke stared at the screen as if stricken.

A rare and legendary talisman. The book is said by some to not even exist. First written on flesh, then stone, and then on indestructible parchment. It is rumored to contain every evil curse and spell in the universe.

The circle winked out.

The weight of silence filled the room.

T'Challa felt as if he could hear his own heartbeat. A feeling of dread settled over his shoulders. The Darkhold, he thought. *Created out of dark matter.*

"That sounds . . . beyond creepy," Zeke said.

"What would Mr. McGuire be doing with this book?" Sheila asked.

T'Challa hesitated.

Stop now, he told himself. *Go any further and you'll get involved in something dangerous.*

"Chthon," Zeke said. "Look for that."

"No," Sheila said immediately. "Maybe . . . maybe we shouldn't."

They all stared at one another.

T'Challa heard his father's voice in his head: *Use the wisdom and judgment you have been taught. Do not let me down.*

But his inner voice had a differing opinion: *We have to keep going. Mr. McGuire's in danger.*

He looked at Zeke and Sheila, apprehension evident on their faces. "If we do this, there's no going back. Are we all in agreement?"

Zeke nodded, and Sheila closed her eyes and did the same.

T'Challa took a deep breath and tapped the screen. "Chthon . . . demon god. Search."

He shook his head. He couldn't believe he was searching for information on something so . . . horrifying.

It only took a moment to return the search result, but to T'Challa, it felt like eons. He didn't realize his hands were clenched into fists until he released them.

Result: Pronounced *ka-thon*. Elder God thought to be as old as the known universe. First practitioner of dark magic. Said to be the father of all evil things in the world. He exists in a dimension not of this world, and cannot take physical form on Earth. Instead, he uses an entity called "the Other" to carry out his desires.

No one spoke.

T'Challa felt as if he had just been sucked into a black hole and was searching for something to hold on to.

"All this stuff really exists?" Zeke asked. "I mean, demon gods and stuff?"

"You saw what we went through last year, Zeke," Sheila said, "fighting that . . . that creature at our school."

T'Challa released a ragged breath. He remembered the encounter more clearly than he wished. "There are a lot of things in the world that people don't know about, Zeke. Things that are kept away from humanity by—"

"Heroes!" Zeke said, and his eyes lit up. "Like . . . like Thor! And . . . um . . . Iron Man! The real one. Not the one in Vulcan Park."

"Earth has always had protectors," T'Challa told his

friends, "keeping people safe from . . . earthly and unearthly threats."

T'Challa knew of a dozen stories that Zeke and Sheila did not. Tales of how his father and other heroes had saved Earth countless times. The King of Wakanda had told him things that would send Zeke's head spinning. But he couldn't tell his friends that. Better to let them remain safe and carefree. For now, at least.

T'Challa was numb. *The Darkhold* sounded like something that could cause great havoc. What would his father do if he knew it had just been stolen? His thoughts rolled around in his brain, searching for answers.

"T'Challa?" Sheila said.

T'Challa turned to her.

"Bob," she said. "Search for Bob."

Zeke smirked. "There has to be a million hits for Bob."

"Not necessarily," T'Challa countered. "Boolean logic should be able to weed out irrelevant and common names."

He touched the screen again. "New search: Bob." He looked at the picture of Bob at Vulcan Park. "Bob the Acrobat, and Bob, the Good Doctor. Utilize Boolean operators."

"Searching," the voice responded.

The trio watched as the circle went from black to red once again.

"This one's gonna take a while," Zeke predicted.

But no sooner than he had spoken, the voice returned the result:

Bob, or Bob, the Good Doctor. Aliases for the Reverend Doctor Michael Ibn al-Hajj Achebe, PhD. Once a poor farmer from the country of Ghudaza, neighbor to Wakanda, he attended Yale University and obtained several degrees. A trained acrobat and martial artist, his true gift is spreading discord and turmoil. Highly skilled in hypnosis, explosives, and oratory, but also unstable, verging on madness. Rumored to have sold his soul to an entity called Mephisto to gain power.

Silence once again descended.

"Mephisto," Zeke said. "That's another name for the devil." He slumped in his chair. "Great."

"What's he even doing here?" Sheila asked. "Bob?"

No one had an answer.

"Told you Bob wasn't his real name," Zeke said.

"Your father," Sheila suddenly put in. "You can ask him what he knows about Bob—or Achebe."

"Or . . . *The Darkhold*," Zeke said quietly, as if saying the name aloud would summon a horde of demons.

A flicker of doubt passed over T'Challa's face. "No. That's the last thing I want to do. If he found out there was some kind of trouble here, he'd probably put me on a plane back home immediately."

T'Challa thought on that a moment. What they were getting into was more important than his vacation, but he also knew that if he went home, Zeke and Sheila might be in even more peril. He was reminded of the question he had asked himself earlier about Wakanda and the civil rights movement. How things could have been different if Wakanda had helped somehow.

Well, he thought. *I'm not going to stand by while my friends are in danger.*

"If Bob really has the book—" Sheila started.

"He has access to every evil spell in the universe," Zeke finished.

T'Challa looked at Zeke and then Sheila. "Only one thing to do," he said.

"What?" Zeke asked.

"We've gotta find that book."

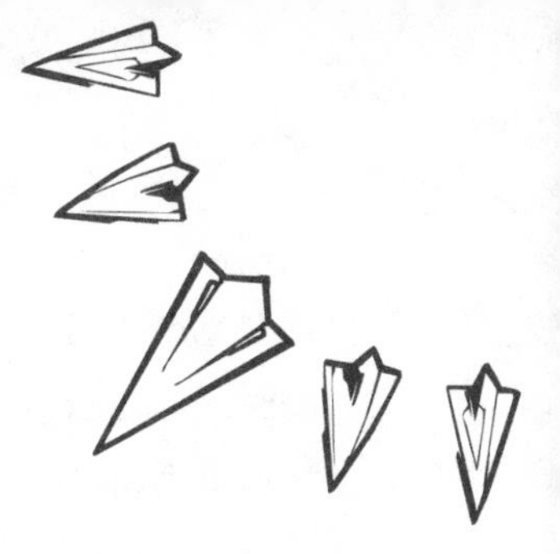

CHAPTER TWELVE

That night, the trio ate as if in a daze. Everything they had learned about *The Darkhold*, Chthon, and Achebe left them rattled. Sheila had insisted on green salads after their past few nights of stuffing themselves with Southern comfort food. Zeke was forlorn and moved the food around on his plate unenthusiastically.

T'Challa speared a fresh cherry tomato from Miss Rose's garden and let it burst in his mouth. It was good to have something fresh and healthy, he realized.

Miss Rose studied all of them intently. "I don't want you kids running around town, okay? I let you go earlier, but I'm still worried. There could be kidnappers out there, looking for who knows what." Her eyes roamed over each one of them, finally landing on T'Challa. "I want you all to stay close to home the next few days, okay, Sheila?"

"We will, Gramma," Sheila said. "We'll be careful."

Miss Rose's gaze rested on her granddaughter. "I'm serious, Sheila. I won't have it. I've seen that same look on your mother. You're both the same. Curious as a cat."

So that's where she gets it, T'Challa thought.

Sheila looked up from her plate and smiled brightly. "No need to worry about me, Gramma," she said. "Honest."

But T'Challa didn't think Miss Rose bought it.

"T'Challa?" Sheila said for the second time.

T'Challa shifted in his chair in Base Camp. His mind was wandering again. Knowing that there was a book out there that could cause such evil left him feeling apprehensive and nervous.

"Sorry. What was that?"

Sheila gave him a concerned look, her mouth quickly tightening.

"The other day, you said you had a dream about Bob—I mean, Achebe—right?"

"Yes," T'Challa replied reluctantly.

Sheila bit her lip, as if she didn't want to say something.

"What?" T'Challa pressed her.

"Well . . . how do you think you fit into all of this? I

mean, he said he would meet you . . . 'where the sand runs like blood.'"

T'Challa shivered at the mysterious phrase.

"If he really did speak to you in your dreams," Zeke added, "he knows who you are."

T'Challa pushed the notion away, although he knew that it was probably true. "What would he want with me?"

He thought back to the state fair and the creepy grin. Achebe had been looking right at him.

He had to do something. Anything. Find Achebe and call him out.

T'Challa sighed. Was he really going to get involved in another escapade like he did on his last visit? His father certainly wouldn't approve.

But . . .

The dream . . .

It had to be telling him something.

If Mr. McGuire was in harm's way, wasn't it T'Challa's duty to help? And if Achebe stole a book that contained every evil spell in the universe, wasn't it up to someone to stop him before he used it?

"I don't know what he would want with you," Sheila said. "But we have to consider it, T'Challa."

"Yeah," Zeke said. "Maybe he followed you here or something."

T'Challa felt his insides flutter. "That's not helping, Zeke."

Zeke shrugged. "Just saying."

"We need a plan," Sheila suggested. "We have to find that book."

"But where?" Zeke countered. "We don't even know where Achebe is, much less the book."

T'Challa thought on what his father would do if he were in his place.

He'd act.

And that's what he decided to do.

T'Challa got up early the next morning and dressed quickly. Zeke was snoring away in the top bunk, totally oblivious to the world. He hoped Sheila was asleep as well. He scribbled a quick note and left it on the dresser: *Going for a run. Be back soon.*

He quietly closed the door behind him and headed for the bathroom.

T'Challa readied himself, brushed his teeth, and washed his face. He'd take a shower later, he told himself. He didn't want anyone being awakened by the gurgling, banging sound of the old pipes in the house, which had woken him up a few times on previous mornings.

He studied his face in the mirror. The faintest wisp of hair brushed his upper lip. He ran his finger along it, wondering if it would ever fill in. "Don't really want a mustache," he whispered aloud. "Maybe a beard one day?"

He turned from the mirror and opened the door.

To be met by the figure of Miss Rose in the hallway.

She held a book in one hand and a cup of steaming coffee in the other.

"T'Challa," she said, surprised. "You're up early."

T'Challa looked to his feet and then back up. "Oh, good morning, Miss Rose. I was just heading out for a run."

Miss Rose studied him. "Remember what I told you kids last night?"

T'Challa gulped. He knew better than to tell even a white lie, but it was too late now. "Yes," he replied.

"I said I didn't want you going far, isn't that right?"

"Yes, ma'am."

T'Challa felt a trickle of sweat on his face.

Miss Rose took a sip of coffee. "You go ahead and take your run, but stay on the main streets, you hear me?"

"Yes, Miss Rose."

Miss Rose looked T'Challa up and down. "You're running in those pants and shoes? Don't you have any workout gear?"

T'Challa swallowed the lump in his throat. "I, um . . . Well, I forgot to bring clothes for that. I'll be fine, though." He smiled. "I can run in anything!"

Miss Rose gave him a skeptical look. "I'm making shrimp and grits for breakfast. So if you want some, you better be back before Zeke wakes up."

T'Challa chuckled, in opposition to his dark mood. "Great. I won't be too long."

Shrimp and grits? he wondered as he headed for the door.

"And be careful!" Miss Rose half shouted.

"I will," he called back.

T'Challa sighed a breath of relief once he closed the door behind him. As if to prove to himself that he didn't just tell a lie, he began to jog at a steady pace. The Alabama sun was already hot, and the heat felt good on his skin. He took deep breaths, giving his lungs a workout. The rhythmic chirp of birds rang in his ears along with the *tik, tik, tik* of water sprinklers nourishing already green lawns. He ran down pleasant tree-lined streets, taking in the sights. Older couples were out for morning walks, and several dogs pulled their owners along eagerly.

T'Challa reached Mr. McGuire's shop and stood out front a moment, catching his breath. He wiped his brow and checked his watch: 8:00 a.m. He peered through the window. The lights were on. A chime rang as he turned the knob and stepped inside.

"Hello?" T'Challa called. "Mika?"

No answer.

T'Challa was once again met by the smell of old leather-bound books. The floorboards creaked as he walked. "Hello?" he called again.

Footsteps sounded near the back of the store.

"Who is there?" a French-accented voice called out. "T'Challa? Is that you?"

T'Challa stepped farther into the store. Mika appeared out of the shadows.

"Mon dieu!" she exclaimed. "You gave me a fright. Why are you here so early?"

"Bonjour, Mika. Je suis désolé. The door was open."

Mika waved her hand in the air. "No need to be sorry, mon ami! I came in early for—how is it called—inventory?" She looked past him. "No Zeke or Sheila?"

"No," T'Challa said. "They're still asleep."

"Ah, sleepyheads, no?"

T'Challa picked up a small elephant that looked as if it was carved from onyx. "No news on Mr. McGuire?"

"Sadly, no," Mika said. "I hope he is okay. He is such a nice man, you know?"

"Right," T'Challa replied. "That's what Sheila told me. I only met him for a few minutes the other day." He gently placed the elephant back on the shelf. "Listen," he began. "That book that was stolen. You said Mr. McGuire found it in Morocco?"

"Oui," Mika replied. "He said it was a long time ago. Maybe five, six years? I do not know for sure."

"Did you ever flip through it or anything?"

Mika shook her head. "No. Monsieur McGuire said I could only touch the cover with gloves, but I never got the chance to look inside." She raised an eyebrow. "You are interested in this book, T'Challa?"

T'Challa shuffled his feet. "Oh, well. Not really. I was just wondering."

There was a moment of silence. T'Challa suddenly felt tongue-tied, at a loss for words. He swallowed. "The man who came in and asked for the book," he continued cautiously. "Did he say anything strange or unusual?"

Mika cocked her head. "Strange? No. Monsieur McGuire told him it was not for sale. I told the police the same thing. This man . . . Bob? He was . . . disappointed when he couldn't buy it, but he left without saying anything else."

"Interesting," T'Challa replied. He had more questions but felt as if he was pressing his luck. Any more and she'd probably get suspicious.

"Well," he said. "I better get back. Sheila's grandmother is making shrimp and grits for breakfast."

"Ah," Mika said. "Fantastique."

T'Challa thanked her and headed for the door.

"Wait!" Mika called out.

T'Challa turned around.

Mika's shoulders rose and fell, as if she was exhaling a long breath. She looked at T'Challa, almost as if stricken. She opened her mouth, but no words came out.

T'Challa took a step forward. "Mika?"

But Mika didn't answer.

Instead, cracks, like dry earth in the desert, appeared on her face. Her eyes flushed a bloodshot red. Not just red, but the red of a thousand blazing suns. She opened her mouth. And this is what she said:

"*The Darkhold* is calling, Young Panther. Are you worthy?"

And then she threw her head back and laughed.

T'Challa froze. Horrified.

"No," he whispered.

He rushed the few steps to Mika and took her by the shoulders. "Mika!" he cried out. "Mika!"

Mika blinked slowly, as if coming back to herself, back from the nightmare that had overcome her. Her maniacal laughter stopped, like a switch had been thrown. Her eyes lost the red glow.

And then she collapsed to the floor.

Mika drank another glass of water. It was her third. "I don't remember anything," she moaned.

Her eyes were clear and bright now, but T'Challa remembered how red they were just moments ago. And her face, like cracked parchment. "Do you remember what you said?" he asked.

Mika shook her head, apparently still disoriented. "Did I say something? I don't remember saying anything."

T'Challa swallowed. *Best to not tell her for now. It might frighten her even more.* "No," he said. "You just cried out."

Mika took another drink of water and then rested her forehead on a closed fist. She was quiet for several long moments. "I'm going to close the shop and go home and get some sleep."

"Good," T'Challa said, helping her up. "That's a good idea."

"I'm glad you were here, T'Challa. If not, I don't know what would have happened."

They locked eyes for a moment until T'Challa turned away, embarrassed.

"C'mon," he said. "Can I walk you to your house?"

"No, merci, my friend. I have a car." She shot him a grin, remarkable considering what had just happened to her. "I'm sixteen, you know."

She grabbed her backpack, and they walked out together. Mika locked the door behind her. "You sure you're okay?" T'Challa asked.

"I'm fine," she said. "Don't worry. It must've been some kind of fainting spell. Papa always tells me I need to eat breakfast instead of just café, so maybe that was it, no?"

"Makes sense," T'Challa said. "Get some rest, and we'll stop by soon to see how you're doing."

Mika paused again, and for a moment, T'Challa froze, thinking that the terrible transformation was about to come over her again. "Mika?" he asked. "Are you okay?"

But Mika didn't immediately answer.

T'Challa tensed.

"I remember now," Mika finally said, a faraway look in her eyes. "This man who came in. Bob. He did say something odd."

T'Challa felt a static charge run along his arms, his senses responding to what was about to come. "What was it?" he asked. "What did he say?"

Mika looked up a moment, and her eyebrows knit together. "It was strange. He said: 'A room without books is like a body without a soul.' "

CHAPTER THIRTEEN

Zeke and Sheila looked up in surprise as T'Challa entered the kitchen. Sunlight poured in through the window, and the smell of spicy cooking filled the air. Miss Rose studied him with a keen eye. "T'Challa," she said. "You're back. How was your . . . *run*?"

T'Challa gulped and wiped nervous sweat from his brow. "Um, just fine."

"You missed shrimp and grits," Zeke said, using his spoon to scoop up the last bite from his bowl.

"I tried to save you some," Sheila said, "but . . ." She nodded in the direction of Zeke, who gave an innocent shrug.

T'Challa tried to maintain his composure, but his mind was still reeling:

The Darkhold *is calling, Young Panther. Are you worthy?*

"Um, I'm gonna grab a quick shower if that's okay?"

"Sure," Miss Rose said. "There are fresh towels in the second bathroom."

"Thanks," T'Challa said, and made his way out of the room. He felt Sheila's eyes on his back as he walked away. He didn't like being untruthful, or even misleading. He saw his father's gaze in his mind's eye, disapproving.

T'Challa turned the water on hot and stepped into the shower. He let it rain down to beat a rhythm over his neck and shoulders. He took deep breaths, trying to erase the bizarre scene of Mika from his mind.

Who could do such a thing? Bob? Was Zeke right? Is he really some sort of supernatural creature?

T'Challa closed his eyes and let the steam fill the whole shower. Even though it was hot outside, and a cool shower would have made more sense, it felt good, and seemed to soak through to his very soul.

Soul.

A room without books is like a body without a soul.

What did it mean?

T'Challa took the stairs to Base Camp slowly. How could he explain what he had just seen to Zeke and Sheila? They'd be terrified. But he had to. There was no way to avoid it.

His friends stared as he entered the room.

"Where'd you go?" Sheila asked before he even reached the bottom step.

"Yeah," Zeke said. "Since when do you go running in the morning?"

T'Challa sat down and fiddled with a pen on the table, his eyes downcast.

"T'Challa?" Sheila ventured, a note of concern in her voice.

"I went to Mr. McGuire's shop," T'Challa confessed, raising his head. "I wanted more answers and asked Mika if she knew anything else."

"Without us?" Zeke said, offended. "We would have gone, too, you know."

"I know," T'Challa replied. "I just felt I needed to go right away. We need answers, and, well, I was up already, and I just had to do something."

"I understand," Sheila said. "What did you discover? Anything?"

T'Challa set the pen down. "I did."

"What was it?" Zeke asked. "A recipe for French toast or something?"

Sheila gave Zeke a side-eye.

T'Challa didn't know what to do with his hands, so he picked up the pen again. "Something . . . something came over Mika."

Sheila leaned in. "What do you mean?"

T'Challa took a deep breath.

"I asked if she knew where Mr. McGuire got the book. *The . . . Darkhold.*"

"And?" Zeke asked.

T'Challa closed his eyes for a brief second. A flash brought the moment back. "Mika suddenly went into some kind of trance. Her eyes were bloodshot and her face . . . changed. She said: '*The Darkhold* is calling, Young Panther. Are you worthy?' "

Sheila and Zeke gasped.

"And then she just . . . fainted," T'Challa finished.

"She fainted?" Sheila said.

"Yes," T'Challa replied. "She's okay now. I helped her up, and she said she didn't remember anything. She wrote it off as not eating enough and drinking too much coffee."

Zeke put his head in his hands. "Now he definitely knows who you are!"

"I know," T'Challa said without emotion. "Don't remind me!"

"Somehow, Achebe had her under his control," Sheila whispered, "if only for a minute."

"But what does it even mean?" T'Challa said, frustrated. "What is Achebe trying to do?"

"That research you did," Zeke started, "with the, um, Boolean thing. It said he was good at hypnosis. Is he hypnotizing people?"

Sheila nodded. "That's a good point, Zeke, but it doesn't explain what happened to Mika. Can hypnosis do that to a person?"

There was a moment of uncomfortable silence. T'Challa fiddled with the pen again. His nerves were rattled, and Sheila picked up on it.

"What else?" she asked. "What else happened?"

T'Challa looked up. *She sure is perceptive,* he thought.

"Well," T'Challa began, "when I asked her if there was anything else she remembered about Achebe, she said she did."

"And?" Sheila asked.

"She said that Achebe told her, 'A room without books is like a body without a soul.'"

A moment passed where no one spoke.

"True," Zeke finally said. "That's a quote from Cicero. You know, the Roman scholar."

Sheila shot Zeke an approving look. "Good one, Zeke."

"Thanks," Zeke said. "Pretty weird thing for Bob—Achebe—to say, though."

"There's something about it that doesn't sit right with me," T'Challa said. "I don't know why. It's just a feeling, like there's a message in there or something."

"We'll find out what it means," Sheila promised, and her eyes narrowed with determination. "We have to."

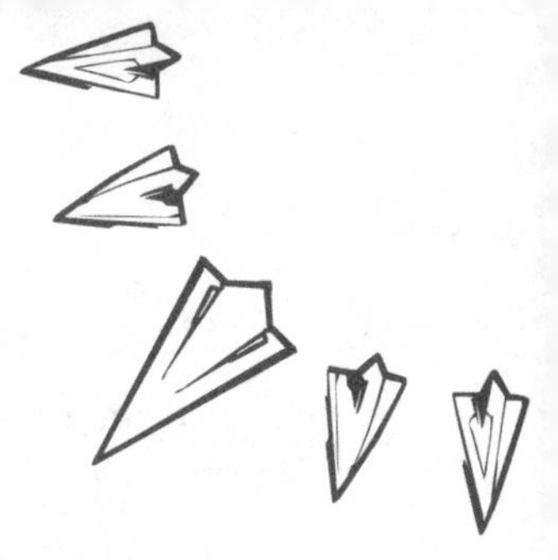

CHAPTER FOURTEEN

Sheila, Zeke, and T'Challa sat around the room and stared at one another, trying to put the pieces together. Every now and then, Miss Rose's footsteps sounded upstairs. The boiler gurgled and belched, making them all jump every time it did so.

"How could Achebe do that to Mika?" Sheila asked the room. "How?"

T'Challa didn't have an answer. A soul was a powerful thing, he knew that much. Every culture in the world, including Wakanda's, had stories and myths about the immortality of the soul. Some even said that it was a tangible thing, something that could actually be seen and felt.

"He has to have some kind of power," Zeke said. "He's a wizard, or, I don't know. A warlock."

"It didn't say anything about that when we did the search," Sheila said, and then began to count on her fingers. "It said he was good at hypnosis, acrobatics, and explosives."

"And firing up a crowd," Zeke added. "Those people at the rally seemed to respond to his speech. Can a spell do that?"

Spell, T'Challa mused.

"Wait a minute," he started. "That research also said he was rumoured to have sold his soul, right?"

Sheila and Zeke both nodded.

"To someone called . . . Mephisto," Zeke said, and then seemed to shrink, as if he wanted to hide under a blanket. T'Challa shook away the fear that was churning in his stomach. He tapped a bead on his Kimoyo Bracelet. Once again, a screen appeared, and he waved it to the wall, where it expanded.

"Search for Achebe, and Mephisto, and"—he looked at Zeke and Sheila—"soul. Text results only."

This time, instead of the automated voice, the screen was flooded with lines of green code. The trio waited as the projection ran through what looked like a cache of a million words and phrases. After a moment, the scrolling text slowed like an old-fashioned car odometer and then stopped. T'Challa stepped up to the screen and read:

"'Achebe, also known as Bob, or the Good Doctor, sold

his soul to Mephisto for power and revenge after his family was murdered by rebels.' "

An emptiness filled the room. T'Challa knew they were all thinking the same thing. "If he sold his soul," he started, "maybe now he wants it back."

" 'A room without books is like a body without a soul,' " Zeke whispered.

"He's speaking about himself!" Sheila said, rising up in her chair a bit.

The room suddenly felt warmer, as if their very words were changing the air around them. "How, though?" Zeke asked. "How does one go about getting a soul?"

"A spell," Sheila said. "And where does one find a ritual like that?" She looked to T'Challa and grinned, as if he already knew the answer.

And that's when T'Challa realized it.

It rang like a bell in his head, bright and clear.

"A book," he said. "One that contains every evil spell in the universe."

He paused. "*The Darkhold*."

No one spoke for a moment, as if they were basking in the relief that they had an answer, or at least one of them.

"But why is he doing this now?" Zeke ventured. "Why here?"

"Did he come all the way here to find the book?" Sheila asked. "And if so, how did he even know it was here? Where did Mr. McGuire get it?"

"Mika said he found it in Morocco," Zeke reminded them. "Remember?"

T'Challa seemed lost in thought. He paused a moment and nodded, as if he was figuring something out before speaking it aloud. "Maybe Bob—Achebe—had been searching for it for a very long time. Years and years, perhaps. He finally traced it to Morocco, and then found that it had been sold to a book dealer in the States."

"Mr. McGuire," Sheila said.

"Exactly," T'Challa replied.

"And we still have no idea where it is," Zeke said, "or how those other phrases fit in: 'where the sand runs like blood' and the other one."

T'Challa shuddered. The Darkhold *is calling, Young Panther. Are you worthy?*

Sheila's phone chimed and she picked it up. "Interesting," she said.

"What?" T'Challa asked.

"I set up alerts for every time *Bob*, *Good Doctor*, or *Achebe* come up on the web."

"What's it say?" asked Zeke.

Sheila brushed a hand through her hair. "'Join the Good Doctor, Bob, for an interactive town hall. Tune in at eight p.m. tomorrow.'"

"What's the website?" Zeke asked.

Sheila scanned over the tablet. "It doesn't have one. You're just supposed to click a link."

“Hmm,” Zeke murmured, leaning back. “Maybe it’s some kind of weird virus that can come through your computer or something.”

“We have no choice,” T’Challa said. “Tomorrow, we’re going to click that link . . . and find out what happens.”

CHAPTER FIFTEEN

The trio stayed close to home the next day. A knot of worry formed in T'Challa's stomach and tightened throughout the afternoon. Tonight, they were going to click the link for Achebe's talk. *Is it foolish to do so?* T'Challa wondered. *Is it all some sort of trap? And how do I play into all of it?*

Young Prince. We will meet where the sand runs like blood.

There were a few things T'Challa knew at this point. One was that Bob—Achebe—was appearing in the same places T'Challa was. Two—he had a connection to Wakanda, being from a neighboring country. And three—somehow, he was showing up in his dreams. It was clear:

Achebe was interested in him, and T'Challa was determined to find out why.

After a quick dinner—another healthy one, to Zeke's chagrin—the trio headed downstairs. It seemed to T'Challa that his vacation was now limited to Base Camp, eating, and sleep.

Zeke picked up a bag of chips and tore into them. Sheila stared at him, shocked. "We just had dinner, Zeke!"

Zeke withdrew his hand from the bag and looked up, crumbs around his mouth. "I need to counteract all that healthy stuff!"

T'Challa suppressed a grin, although it took a little effort.

The time seemed to creep by in seconds as they waited for 8:00 p.m. T'Challa stared around the room, not focusing on anything in particular. He took a sudden interest in an old poster on the wall, undoubtedly left by Miss Rose's sons, which showed a black leopard on a cliff, ready to pounce. T'Challa stared at the poster. Was he the leopard or the prey below?

Zeke ate his chips and bounced his right leg up and down in a nervous gesture. Sheila's index finger hovered over the link on her tablet.

"Okay," T'Challa said. "It's almost time. Let's see what this is all about."

Sheila looked at T'Challa and then Zeke. "Here goes," she said, and clicked the link.

The three of them waited in hushed anticipation.

After a moment, a web page appeared with a picture of Achebe on a wavy red background.

"'Your host will be with you shortly,'" Sheila read.

"We should record it," Zeke suggested. "Just in case we need to study whatever he's going to say."

"Good idea, Zeke" Sheila said.

"Here," T'Challa put in, and hovered his wrist over Sheila's tablet. The web page rose from her screen in a funnel shape and, somehow, squeezed itself into one of T'Challa's beads. From there, he tapped the bead once, which made the image reappear on the wall.

"I'll never get tired of that," Zeke confessed.

Sheila set her tablet close by and pressed Record.

A burst of white light filled the screen. T'Challa and his friends flinched, raising their hands to cover their eyes.

"What the—?" Zeke cried out.

T'Challa peeked through his fingers. "It's gone," he said. "The light."

"That was weird," Sheila said.

"You think?" Zeke fired back, blinking furiously.

"I hate that phrase," Sheila declared. "*Ya think?* It's like an insult or something. Ugh."

"Shhh!" T'Challa whisper-shouted.

The white light, now dim, revealed Achebe sitting at a desk. The red background was revealed to be a curtain, rippling slowly as if stirred by a breeze. Achebe's hands were folded in front of him, and his back was ramrod straight.

"That's odd," Zeke said. "The whole vibe. Just looks weird."

"I know," Sheila said.

"Welcome," Achebe greeted his virtual audience.

The camera zoomed in closer to Achebe's face. A little too close, T'Challa noticed.

"You can see the red in his eyes," Zeke said. "Creepy."

Red, T'Challa remembered. *Bloodred, like Mika's eyes.*

"I wish to speak to the citizens of Beaumont today," Achebe started. "Just you and me. I wish to talk about . . . sacrifice."

"Sacrifice?" Sheila repeated. "What's he talking about?"

Achebe stared dead into the camera. "No, not that type of sacrifice . . ."

Sheila exchanged a frightened glance with T'Challa.

"I'm speaking about a sacrifice of one's *will* . . . to give yourself truly to a cause."

Achebe's voice was calm and measured. Neither loud nor soft, but something in between, a tone that lured you in, word by word.

He reached for an object just out of camera range. When he pulled it back into the frame, T'Challa saw that it was an art object of some sort, one with a metal stand and two steel balls on a wire that clacked rhythmically against each other.

Click, clack, click, clack. It reminded him of the metronome he used when learning piano.

"Now," Achebe continued, clasping his hands back together. "I believe there is a great need in the world today. A need for those willing to stand up. That is the purpose of Rising Souls."

Click, clack, click, clack.

T'Challa was fixated on Achebe's face. He remembered the dream and the maniacal laughter and felt his head grow dizzy.

"The world today is crying out," Achebe said, his voice calm and steady, every syllable falling in time with the sound of the clacking balls.

"This seems weird," Zeke said, blinking slowly. "My head feels funny."

"There are so many lost souls out there," Achebe went on, his red eyes wide open. "People who need a cause, something to devote their lives to. I am here to deliver you. A higher cause awaits. Come with me . . . listen. I will call on you. Wait for my voice. . . ."

Click, clack, click, clack.

T'Challa rubbed his brow. "Something's going on," he said. "Something . . ."

Click, clack, click, clack.

"Turn it off," Sheila said, clamping her hands over her ears.

T'Challa felt a wave of calm spread through his body,

like the hot-stone massage he had once received after a long run. Every doubt and fear of his began to melt away. He felt as if he were being pulled along by a strong current, farther and farther out to sea.

And then Achebe said a word. A word none of them had ever heard before. A word that slipped from his mouth like the forked tongue of a snake.

“Solstitium,” Achebe whispered slowly, enunciating each syllable, his eyes never blinking. “*Sol-stit-i-um . . .*”

“Turn it off!” Sheila shouted.

T’Challa jerked awake.

He stood up. For a moment, he didn’t know where he was, but then he saw Sheila covering her ears and Zeke lounging back in his chair as if he had fallen asleep, mouth wide open. He quickly tapped the bead, and the image of Achebe blinked off.

There was a moment of silence.

“You okay?” T’Challa asked the room.

Zeke scratched his head, coming awake. Sheila exhaled heavily.

“What happened?” Zeke said.

“Achebe,” T’Challa said in a breathless whisper. “He tried to hypnotize us.”

CHAPTER SIXTEEN

"Okay," Zeke said. "Now we know for *sure* he's a creepy villain."

T'Challa sat down heavily.

"At least we had the good sense to turn it off," Zeke said.

"We?" Sheila shot back. "I think *I* was the first one to snap out of it."

"Well," Zeke countered, "*I* was the one who said my head felt funny before you said *that*."

"Guys!" T'Challa shouted.

Zeke and Sheila quaked at T'Challa's outburst. He didn't raise his voice often, and they both knew it was a sign of his worry and frustration.

"What about the *other* people who were watching?" T'Challa asked. "We couldn't have been the only ones. Did they turn it off? *That's* the question."

"Problem, you mean," Sheila said quietly.

"That's why he held that rally," Zeke said. "So he could get people to trust him and click that link."

"I think Zeke's right," Sheila said. "Remember what that research said? It said he was a good speaker, an orator."

"And that he liked spreading turmoil," Zeke added, still rubbing his brow.

T'Challa fingered the beads on his bracelet. "He has *The Darkhold*—we think—and now he's trying to hypnotize people."

"And Mr. McGuire's still missing," Sheila added.

"Oh man," Zeke said. "What are we gonna do?"

"I don't know," said T'Challa, "but we have to do something. And quickly."

The trio stayed up past midnight, racking their brains for any more clues, but none came. T'Challa was crestfallen. He was the son of the Black Panther. Shouldn't he be able to come up with a plan?

"Solstitium," Sheila whispered. "That word. Did you hear it?"

Zeke rubbed his forehead again. "All I remember is the white light. I feel . . . tired."

T'Challa cast a worried glance at Zeke. "I remember. Solstitium. What does it mean? I've never heard it before."

Sheila shrugged. "Me either."

Zeke looked up, shock etched on his face. He peered at T'Challa and then Sheila. "Wait a minute. Did I hear that correctly? Sheila doesn't know the definition of a word?" He mock-slapped his forehead. "Someone mark the date!"

Sheila managed a weak smile despite the strangeness of it all. She whipped out her phone.

"Hmm," she said after a moment. "Solstice comes from the Latin word solstitium. *Sol* is sun and *sistere* is to stand still. Ancient astronomers called it the day"—she furrowed her brow and looked up—"when the sun stands still?"

The boiler belched, making all of them jump in their chairs.

"What in the world does that mean?" Zeke asked.

"Solstice," Sheila whispered, and scrolled through her phone once more.

"What are you looking for?" T'Challa asked, but Sheila didn't answer. He had seen her like this before. Once she set her mind to something, there was no way to interrupt. "Here it is," she finally said.

"What?" both T'Challa and Zeke asked.

"The summer solstice," Sheila read, "takes place on June twentieth."

“That’s like five days away or something,” T’Challa said.

A sudden realization seemed to dawn on all of them.

“Achebe has something planned,” T’Challa said. “And he’s doing it on the summer solstice.”

CHAPTER SEVENTEEN

T'Challa focused on the swirling colors of the lava lamp. Round globules of red, yellow, and green broke off and came back together again, like a cell dividing over and over. Earlier, as he, Zeke, and Sheila had tried to stay awake and make more connections, one by one their heads began to nod, until finally, they all retired to bed. . . .

T'Challa peered around the strange place he found himself in. It was dark—darker than a starless night. He didn't know where he was, but he knew it was someplace he didn't want to be.

A feeling of dread and loneliness filled his being.

He reached out a hand, trying to feel his way through the

murk, but there was nothing there to give any indication of where he was. The ground beneath his feet was solid, but soft, almost as if he were walking on sand.

"Hello?" he called, and his voice bounced back in his ears.

"Young Panther," a voice called.

T'Challa froze.

It was more of a thought than a voice, he realized, as if someone had spoken to him inside his head.

"This way," the phantom spoke. "Come to me."

T'Challa didn't want to, but somehow, he put one foot in front of the other, as if he had no choice, and began to walk very, very slowly, one step at a time.

Something drove him forward. A great desire, but he didn't know for what.

A few more steps and he found himself in a room where light shone down from an unseen roof. A black pedestal stood ahead of him, about four feet tall. Something sat atop it, a shape.

T'Challa paused, trying to focus, but he couldn't. He just had to keep moving forward.

"Come," the voice inside his head beckoned.

T'Challa halted before the pedestal. The hair stood up on the back of his neck. His heart raced furiously. He looked down.

It was a book.

A book like he had never seen before. The cover, if one could call it that, was iron gray, with small symbols at each corner. Most disturbing, and the thing that made him shudder, was the agonized faces depicted in openmouthed, silent screams. They shifted and moved, twisted and turned, as if trapped in a murky swamp of despair.

"Open me," the voice called. "Turn the page."

T'Challa reached out a trembling hand . . .

A flash of white bolted T'Challa up out of bed, his breath coming fast.

He was safe. Only dreaming.

His breathing slowed. "A book," he whispered. "*The Darkhold*."

Zeke's snores above him sounded loudly in his ears—a reassuring, if annoying, sound.

T'Challa tried to remember everything about the dream, but all he could recall was a suffocating darkness and a cold voice that called out to him.

It was Achebe. Why tell me to open the book?

T'Challa sighed and settled back into bed. A slice of moonlight shone in through the window.

Before he knew it, he was once again asleep.

T'Challa felt the headache before he even opened his eyes, a throbbing in his skull that traveled down to his neck and shoulder blades. He yawned and climbed out of bed, then knocked on the bottom platform of the top bunk. "Wake up, sleepyhead."

No answer.

"Zeke?" T'Challa said, taking the first few steps of the

ladder to the top bunk. Nothing but rumpled sheets. *Must be downstairs,* he thought.

The smell of blueberry pancakes and bacon led him to the kitchen, where Miss Rose and Sheila were already digging in. “Morning,” T’Challa said.

“About time you got up,” Sheila said. “Where’s Zeke? I thought the smell of food would wake him up.”

T’Challa scratched his head. “Zeke? I thought he was down here. He’s not upstairs.”

Miss Rose shook her head. “I’ve been down here since six thirty, and I haven’t seen him.”

Sheila tapped her fork against the edge of her plate. “Maybe he went for a walk or something.”

But T’Challa knew better.

Something was wrong.

Something bad had happened to Zeke.

CHAPTER EIGHTEEN

Sheila dragged T'Challa out of the kitchen and into the basement when Miss Rose got up to make more coffee.

"I didn't want her to freak out," she whispered. "We have to find him. Like, *now*!"

"Where could he have gone off to?" T'Challa asked.

"I don't know, but I'm worried. He's not the type to just run off without telling us. It has something to do with last night. I know it does. That video from Achebe. I knew we shouldn't have watched it!"

T'Challa didn't want to think the worst, but the timing was just too precise. They listen to a weird hypnotic message and then one of them goes missing that night? It couldn't be coincidence.

T'Challa sighed heavily. "Sheila," he started. "I had a dream last night. It was weird. I felt like—"

"T'Challa," Sheila said, looking straight into his eyes. "Zeke is missing. You can tell me about the dream later. Okay?"

T'Challa nodded, embarrassed. Sheila was right. Zeke was missing, and that was the most important thing at the moment. He wished he could have taken it back. "I didn't even hear him get out of bed. How could he have just disappeared?"

Sheila's face showed her distress. "I think Achebe is behind it. I just have a bad feeling."

The idea that Zeke was in real danger suddenly dawned on T'Challa. He could be hurt, or worse. "We have to do something," he said, his voice almost frantic. "We can't just sit here!"

"I know," Sheila said. "I'm thinking!"

T'Challa winced at Sheila's outburst. He had never seen her so worried. He suddenly realized just how much Zeke meant to her. As much as they argued and teased each other, they were the best of friends.

"Let me try calling him first," Sheila suggested, calming down a little. "He's always attached to his phone. Maybe he's not missing at all."

T'Challa nodded but was pretty sure that Zeke wasn't just out for a morning stroll.

Sheila scrolled through her phone and dialed Zeke's number. She put it on speaker. One ring. Two rings. Three. T'Challa's heart felt heavier with each unanswered ring. Four. Sheila finally hung up.

Several minutes passed where neither of them spoke. T'Challa racked his brain for an answer. "We better come up with a plan soon," Sheila said, "before Gramma gets too worried. We have to find him!"

T'Challa fiddled with the beads on his Kimoyo Bracelet, thinking. "Wait," he said.

"What?" Sheila exclaimed, eager.

"I can try to track him."

"With what?"

"This," T'Challa said. He tapped a bead on his bracelet, and the small screen appeared. With a flick of the wrist, it floated to the wall and expanded. "Tracking," he said, after reading Zeke's number aloud.

"Unbelievable," Sheila whispered. "You can actually track with just a number?"

"Yup," T'Challa replied, not taking his eyes off of the monitor. "The techs in Wakanda are amazing."

"I'm sure *that's* an understatement," Sheila replied.

Hundreds of scrolling numbers ran down the screen in green type. T'Challa and Sheila waited without speaking. The numbers slowed. There was a beep, and then a voice:

Location found. Vulcan Park, Red Mountain, Alabama. Coordinates 32.3182° N, 86.9023° W.

T'Challa turned to Sheila. "What in the world?"

"What's he doing in Vulcan Park?" Sheila asked.

"I don't know," T'Challa replied, "but we need to go there. Now!"

"We think we know where he is, Gramma," Sheila said as they headed for the door. "We're gonna go get him. His phone must have died."

Miss Rose set down her coffee cup. "And where do you think he is?"

Sheila swallowed loudly. "Um, we think he's at Red Mountain."

"Red Mountain?" Miss Rose said. "What in the world's he doing there so early?"

"Not sure," Sheila answered. "But I think that's where he is."

The doubt was clear on Miss Rose's face. "Hmpf," she snorted. "Well, he *better* be there. If you don't find him, I'm calling the police."

"I know," Sheila said. "I'm sure he's okay."

T'Challa tried to put on a face that didn't show his distress, as if Zeke disappearing in the middle of the night was something he did all the time. He wasn't sure it worked, though, as Miss Rose gave him a curious stare before they headed out the door. "Be careful," she called to their retreating backs. "And come straight home!"

T'Challa and Sheila barely spoke on the bus ride to Red Mountain.

T'Challa peered through the window. His head was filled with so many questions fighting for attention:

Is Zeke safe?

How did he get to Red Mountain?

What does Achebe want with him?

T'Challa remembered the cold voice: *Open me. Turn the page.*

Harsh sunlight fell across the backrest in front of him, creating rays of slanting light. *Solstitium,* he thought. *Summer solstice. What is Achebe planning?*

Sheila nudged him. "T'Challa. Almost there."

T'Challa came back to himself. He looked out of the grimy bus window and saw the wavy haze of heat rising from the black asphalt. The bus came to a stop with a groaning hiss of pistons. Outside, the park was full of tourists, just as T'Challa remembered from his first visit. The Vulcan statue stood tall and proud, looking out over its domain, iron spear in hand. T'Challa was reminded of how Achebe had climbed up it and set sail, arms outstretched like a bird in flight.

"What now?" Sheila asked, looking around.

"We need to find those exact coordinates," T'Challa said.

He looked around warily and tapped a bead on his wrist. A 3D holographic image appeared and hovered in the air in front of him. GPS coordinates ran along the bottom edge. He covered the small floating screen with his free hand.

"This way," he said.

They walked southeast, and T'Challa kept his eye on the small screen hovering above his wrist.

"Strange," T'Challa said, stopping on the path.

"What?"

"It leads out of the park." He looked up from the hologram. "Out that way, toward the mountains."

"That *is* strange," Sheila said. "Why would he be all the way out there?"

"I don't know," T'Challa replied, growing more anxious with every step he took.

Sunlight glinted off the tall treetops ahead of them as T'Challa and Sheila made their way out of the park. T'Challa continued to peer at the map as they walked. Sheila took a swig of water from a thermos and handed it to T'Challa, who also drank.

The landscape was now rocks and red dirt. The cry of a hawk or falcon sounded in T'Challa's ears, and he looked up to see a massive bird with an enormous wingspan circling in the air.

Sheila raised her head and shaded her eyes. "That's a vulture," she said ominously. "A carrion eater."

T'Challa didn't reply.

They walked for a few more minutes in silence. T'Challa turned around. The park was distant now, but Vulcan could still be seen, an iron giant standing tall.

The hot Alabama sun beat down on their backs, and T'Challa wiped sweat from his brow. After another ten minutes' walk, the mouth of a cave loomed ahead of them, dark and foreboding. Sheila jumped as a voice announced:

Coordinates match. Location found.

Sheila and T'Challa shared uneasy glances.

"In there?" Sheila ventured. "This is an old mine."

"I suppose so," T'Challa replied. He was nervous, but they had to go in. There was no way around it. He tapped a bead, and the projection winked out. *Should have brought the suit,* he told himself. *Zeke's in there, and Bast knows what else.*

"The sign," Sheila said, pointing to their left. "It says 'No Entrance. Danger.'"

T'Challa looked at the rusted and bullet-riddled sign. "Well," he said. "They're right. It *is* dangerous, but our friend's in there."

Sheila's shoulders rose and fell.

And they both stepped inside.

Immediately, damp air caressed both of their faces. T'Challa resisted the urge to shout Zeke's name. He raised his hand in front of his face—darkness.

"I can't see where I'm going," Sheila said.

T'Challa felt his wrist for a Kimoyo bead and tapped it. A beam of light appeared and then spilled along the cave floor.

"That bracelet sure comes in handy," Sheila said. "Better than a cell phone flashlight."

T'Challa looked along the ground where he was walking. To his left, a signpost read: ISHKOODA NUMBER 14 MINE. 1895 TO 1941. "What's that all about?" he asked.

"Remember how I told you my granddaddy used to work in the mines?" Sheila said. "It was here. They used to dig for iron ore."

T'Challa nodded as he walked in the dark, the light from his Kimoyo Bracelet providing a visible path. Their footsteps echoed in his ears. A drop of water splashed on T'Challa's shoe. He looked up. Stalactites clung to the ceiling like giant icicles. A steady drip of water pinged in his ears.

"What are we gonna do," Sheila said quietly, "if Achebe is in here somewhere?"

No sooner had she spoken than T'Challa heard a sound, and his stomach pitched. "Did you hear that?" he asked, his voice fearful.

"No," Sheila said. "What was it?"

T'Challa didn't have to answer.

A moan escaped from the surrounding darkness.

Sheila looked around nervously.

"This way!" T'Challa said. "It's coming from over here!"

He darted left and ran down the tunnel.

"Wait!" Sheila cried behind him.

T'Challa came to a stop, and Sheila skidded alongside him, spraying mud.

"There!" Sheila pointed, breathing hard. "What's that?"

T'Challa followed her finger in the dark.

A bulky shape lay ahead of them, sprawled on the ground, arms outstretched.

"Oh my god!" Sheila whispered.

T'Challa, with all the bravery he could summon, walked toward the shape.

As they drew closer, they saw with horror what it was.

Zeke, lying facedown in a shallow puddle of water.

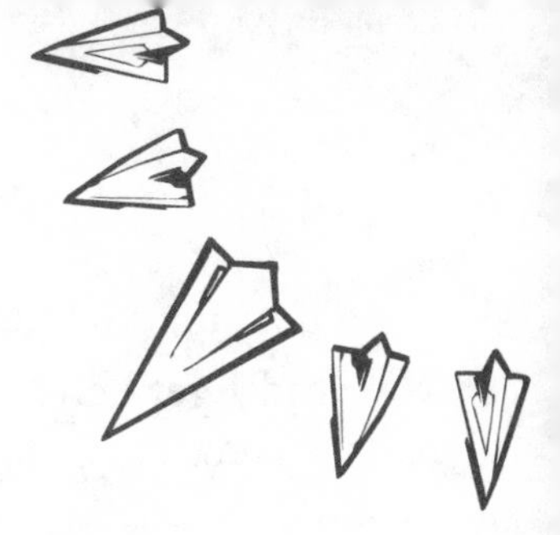

CHAPTER NINETEEN

"Zeke!" T'Challa pleaded. "Wake up!"

Sheila helped turn him over. His clothes were damp from the small puddle of murky cave water, and his eyes were cloudy.

"Zeke," T'Challa said again.

Zeke looked at the both of them for a long moment, as if he had never seen them before, until, finally, recognition dawned in his eyes. "Sheila? T'Challa?"

T'Challa exhaled a relieved breath. "Can you stand?"

"I think so," Zeke groaned.

T'Challa and Sheila helped him up, one of them on each shoulder. Zeke looked around the dark cave with wide eyes.

Dirt marked his face. "What . . . is this place? How . . . how did I get here?"

"We were hoping you could tell us that," Sheila told him.

A half hour later, Zeke was back home with his friends. Miss Rose squeezed him in a bear hug so tightly, he felt like he couldn't breathe.

"Where were you, child?" Miss Rose asked, breaking the embrace.

T'Challa froze where he stood.

They were so caught up in the fact that Zeke was safe, they forgot to get their story straight on the bus ride home. Plus, Zeke was asleep most of the way back.

Zeke's blank-faced stare was obvious.

Sheila jumped in immediately. "Wouldn't you know it?" she said, a little too eagerly. "Red Mountain, just like I said."

Miss Rose pressed her lips into a thin line. "And what were you doing there so early?"

Zeke fidgeted, clearly at a loss for words. T'Challa felt for him but didn't know what to say.

Zeke looked down at his feet and then back up. His face was pained. He opened his mouth but then closed it again. "I just . . . felt like going," he finally managed to say.

Miss Rose crossed her arms. "Your shoes are all wet. How'd that happen? Hasn't rained since you've been here."

"He's tired, Gramma," Sheila said, coming to Zeke's

rescue, which was clearly needed. "Let's just give him some time to rest. Okay?"

"Mmm-hmm," Miss Rose murmured. She looked her granddaughter up and down, and her expression grew even more agitated. "Sheila. Where in tarnation have you been, child? You've got mud all over you!"

Tarnation? T'Challa wondered. *Never heard that one before.*

Sheila looked down at the mud on her jeans and then raised her head. For once, she was speechless.

"You children better keep yourselves out of trouble," Miss Rose warned them. "I'm not playing!"

"Yes, ma'am," Sheila said.

T'Challa took Sheila's lead as well. "Yes, ma'am. We will."

"Good," Miss Rose declared, and gave them all a withering look before she walked away.

T'Challa exhaled, glad to be out of her crosshairs.

After Zeke got cleaned up, the trio headed downstairs to Base Camp.

Zeke flopped onto the couch. "I'm sorry," he said to no one in particular. "I didn't want to lie to Miss Rose."

"Of course you didn't," Sheila said. "But . . . you *can* tell us." She sat down at the table and rested her chin on her closed fists. "Now. What happened? Why'd you leave in the middle of the night?"

Zeke looked at Sheila and then T'Challa.

"I don't know," he said, and his face was distraught. "I don't remember!"

"Nothing?" T'Challa asked.

Zeke shook his head.

T'Challa looked Zeke over, searching for any sign of injury. "Are you hurt?"

"No. Just . . . tired. Like I could sleep for days. Head hurts a little, too."

"You've got to remember *something*," Sheila said.

Zeke paused, clearly befuddled. He was silent for several long moments. T'Challa and Sheila exchanged nervous looks, concerned for their friend.

Zeke finally broke his silence. "I just remember this voice in my head telling me to go outside."

"So you *do* remember something," Sheila said, encouraged. "What kind of voice? Was it Achebe?"

Zeke scrunched up his face. "I don't know. I think so. I don't remember."

"And then what did you do?" T'Challa asked.

Zeke sighed, frustrated. "Well, I remember climbing down the little ladder from the top bunk. You were sleeping. I remember looking at you, but for some reason, I couldn't say anything. It was like . . . like I wasn't able to snap out of it."

T'Challa felt a sudden chill.

"After that," Zeke continued, "I don't remember anything, just waking up where you found me."

T'Challa heard footsteps.

The door at the top of the steps opened.

T'Challa tensed.

A step creaked.

And then another.

T'Challa raised a finger to his lips. "Shhh."

He stood up quietly and crept out of the direct line of sight. He waited, keeping an eye on Zeke's and Sheila's faces.

Another step creaked.

T'Challa tensed, ready to leap into action.

A relieved smile formed on Sheila's face.

Miss Rose came down the bottom step. "Thought you could use something to eat, Zeke. I know you can't go more than twenty minutes without a meal."

T'Challa exhaled and came out from around the side of the stairway.

"Thank you, Miss Rose," Zeke said.

"Ham-and-cheese sandwich, chips, and a soda," Miss Rose pointed out, setting down the plate. "That should keep you out of trouble for a while."

"Thanks, Gramma," Sheila said.

"Hmpf," Miss Rose murmured, looking around the room like she was seeing it for the first time. "What are you kids doing down in this musty old basement, anyway?"

T'Challa gulped.

"Nothing," Sheila said. "It's too hot to always sit outside, you know?"

Miss Rose gave her that look—the one T'Challa had already seen on several occasions.

"Uh-huh," Miss Rose said, doubtful. "Not gonna tell you kids again to be careful with yourselves. Got that? Not after this child here wandered off. You hear me?"

They all answered with a nod and contrite faces. Miss Rose took one last look around and headed back upstairs.

T'Challa sat back down, his nerves still on edge. He heard the door at the top of the steps close.

"Well, he hasn't lost his appetite," Sheila quipped, turning back to Zeke, who had already consumed half his sandwich. "What about Mr. McGuire? Did you see him?"

Zeke was sitting up on the couch now, his eyes a bit clearer. He swallowed another bite and chewed very slowly for a long, long time, which made Sheila give an exhausted sigh.

"I didn't see him," Zeke finally said.

"It just doesn't add up," T'Challa said, sitting back. "How do you think you got there? In that cave?"

"I couldn't've walked there," Zeke said, scratching his head as if he'd find an answer there. "It's too far away." He suddenly gave them both a frightened look. "Don't tell me I actually got on a bus! Like a sleepwalker or something!"

Neither T'Challa nor Sheila spoke for a moment.

"Achebe had to have hypnotized you somehow," Sheila said quietly.

Zeke looked at her, alarmed.

"Last night," T'Challa said. "That video."

"Oh," Zeke said. "That's right. I knew there was something weird about it. What about you guys? How come you didn't get . . . hypnotized? If that's even what happened."

Sheila nodded along to Zeke's question. "I think, from what I've read, a certain type of person is more susceptible to hypnosis than others. People taken with . . . flights of fancy are more easily influenced."

"Like me," Zeke said.

Sheila nodded.

"Plus," T'Challa said, "Sheila had her hands over her ears when the video was playing, and she's probably too—"

"Too what?" Sheila cut him off.

T'Challa searched for the right words. He didn't want to say the wrong thing. "Well, I guess maybe you're too much of a skeptic to be influenced."

"Perhaps," Sheila said, proving his point.

"What about you, T'Challa?" Zeke asked. "How come you didn't walk out of the house at three a.m. or whatever time it was?"

T'Challa thought on that a moment. "Well," he started. "I don't really know. I knew something odd was happening, so maybe my brain put up a defense mechanism of some sort."

Sheila took a long look at Zeke. "Why would Achebe get you to go all the way out to the cave and then just . . . leave you there?"

"He wanted us to find you," T'Challa said. "That's the only reason I can think of."

Could it be true? he wondered. *Was this all some sort of trap?*

Zeke took a drink of soda and set it on the table. "I remember the dark, and voices." He squeezed his fists together, irritated. "I can't remember! I really can't! It's right in the back of my brain, but I can't bring it to the front!"

"What about the book?" T'Challa asked. "*The Darkhold.* Did you see or hear anything about that?"

Zeke raised his head. "No. Nothing about that. I remember a shape that could have been a man, but I had a hard time focusing. Like I was under a spell or something." He rubbed his forehead. "I'm tired," he said, yawning. He pushed his plate away. "Enough questions. I need some sleep."

"Okay, Zeke," T'Challa said in a reassuring tone. "You get some rest."

"Yeah," Sheila replied. "Get some sleep and we'll talk later."

Zeke didn't answer, but put his head back and closed his eyes.

▲▲▲

T'Challa and Sheila sat outside while Zeke got some much-needed rest. Warm rays of sunlight bathed the yard in golden light. Two cardinals chirped and flitted between the hanging flower baskets, and T'Challa watched them with a smile—a rare moment, he suddenly realized.

"Just doesn't make sense," he said, more to himself than to Sheila.

"I know," Sheila replied.

They didn't speak again for a long moment, only sat together and wandered in their own meandering thoughts.

"Listen," T'Challa finally began. "That dream I was going to tell you about . . ."

The back screen door banged open, and T'Challa jumped in his chair.

It was Zeke. "I remember!" he shouted, waving his arms in the air. "I remember something else!"

CHAPTER TWENTY

"What?" T'Challa asked, his nerves suddenly jumping. "What is it?"

Zeke closed his eyes a moment, as if dredging up a memory he'd rather forget. "I remembered when I fell asleep just now. It came back to me. Two people were arguing. I heard them, but I couldn't see their faces. One of them had a weird, high-pitched voice and was telling the other one to shut up, that he knew what he was doing. I think I heard the name . . . Daki."

"Daki?" T'Challa said, his voice a question mark.

"Yeah," Zeke went on. "Daki. And then someone said

that word—that word we heard when Achebe was doing his web thing. Sol . . . sun . . . ?" He trailed off.

"Solstitium?" Sheila ventured.

Zeke clapped his hands together. "Right! Solstitium." He mumbled to himself, as if trying to recall more. "'Solstitium,' the voice said. 'The solstitium is . . . near.'"

Sheila closed her eyes and opened them again. "The summer solstice," she said.

T'Challa exhaled. All the clues were coming together, but he still didn't know how they were connected. "There's something I need to tell you guys," he started, "and I'm only just now getting the chance."

Sheila and Zeke waited while T'Challa stood up and paced back and forth, nervously rubbing his hands together. "I had another dream last night. I told you about the one where I saw Achebe and heard his voice. But in this one, I was in a cold, dark place, like . . . like the cave we found you in, Zeke." He paused. His mouth was dry. "I saw a book."

"*The* book?" Sheila asked.

"I think so," T'Challa said. "But that's not all. It was sitting on a pedestal of some sort, like it was put there for me. And then I heard a voice say, 'Open me. Turn the page.'"

Zeke gulped. "Now *The Darkhold* is talking to you? In your *dreams*?"

T'Challa reeled at the prospect of Achebe knowing who he was. Why was he tempting him with *The Darkhold*?

"What do we do now?" Zeke asked.

Zeke and Sheila both looked at T'Challa.

T'Challa released a deep, weighted sigh.

They're looking to me for help, like I have all the answers.

But he didn't. Not this time.

That evening, after dinner, the trio retreated to the backyard to sit in the open air. The heat from the Alabama sun was lessened somewhat by slowly darkening clouds. Miss Rose suggested putting out some citronella Tiki torches to keep the mosquitoes away, which Zeke offered to do. Now they sat and watched trails of wispy, lemon-scented smoke drift in the air around them.

Zeke used a brush to scrub the mud from his sneakers. Fine red dirt fell to the ground at his feet, forming a little mound. T'Challa stared at it, fascinated.

"Why are you staring at my shoes?" Zeke asked.

"I'm not looking at your shoes," T'Challa told him. "I'm looking at the dirt."

"Interesting," Zeke said. "Well, let me know what you discover."

Sheila looked up from her research.

"The dirt," T'Challa said. "It looks more like . . . sand. *Red* sand."

Zeke glanced at Sheila as if T'Challa were speaking a language he didn't understand. "Like . . . *blood*," T'Challa continued.

Zeke's mouth formed an O.

"Where the sand runs like blood," Sheila said. Her eyes lit up. "Iron ore! That's what they used to mine in the caves! The dust from iron ore gives the soil a reddish tint." She paused and then swallowed, as if she couldn't get the words out quickly enough. "It's the place where Achebe said he would meet you, T'Challa."

Could it be? T'Challa wondered. They didn't have a lot of time to wait and find out. The solstice was fast approaching. "We have to go back," he said quietly.

"What?" Zeke said, but T'Challa was pretty certain his friend had heard him the first time.

"We have to go back," he repeated. "To the cave."

Zeke's refusal was clear as he shook his head back and forth. "Nope. Nope. Nope."

"We'll be careful," Sheila said. "We'll make sure nothing happens to you again. It's our best shot. That's where you heard Achebe talking, right? Plus, Mr. McGuire might be there, too."

"I don't know who I heard," Zeke said. "All I heard were the voices and someone being called . . . Daki, whoever that is."

"Zeke," T'Challa said, drawing closer. "We've got your back. I swear I'll protect you as best I can. Promise."

I hope I can, T'Challa thought. *I know I can.*

Zeke stared at both of his friends, his expression now unreadable. He rubbed his neck. "Well," he finally said, "if you guys think that's what we need to do, I'm in." His frown slowly turned into a weak smile. "T'Challa?" he asked, a sincere note in his voice.

"Yeah?"

"Can I wear your suit?"

"No," T'Challa said, almost laughing.

Almost.

They all sat in silence for a long time, as if their decision to go back to the cave had sent them into some sort of shock where they could no longer speak. T'Challa peered up at the moon, barely visible at this point. He thought of his father back home and realized he had never spoken to him, only Shuri. He hoped she had given him the message that he had arrived safely. That was one thing he had promised before he left Wakanda—that he would stay in touch on a regular basis.

"Be right back," he said, and walked over to the far side of the yard, where a rickety fence had been strangled by tough, creeping vines. "Here goes," he said aloud, and tapped a bead on his Kimoyo Bracelet. A small screen hovered above the bead, wavering in the night air. After a moment, his father, T'Chaka, the Black Panther and King of Wakanda, appeared.

"Father," T'Challa said, a tone of reverence in his voice. One couldn't help but address the Black Panther with admiration and respect. He commanded it by his presence alone, even if he was thousands of miles away.

"T'Challa!" his father exclaimed. "About time you checked in. How are you and your friends?"

T'Challa turned his body away from the kitchen window, just in case Miss Rose was looking out at the backyard.

"I'm good. It's great to see Zeke and Sheila again."

His father smiled, which was something that didn't happen often, and T'Challa savored the moment. He struggled with what to say next. Should he ask about Achebe? *The Darkhold*?

Fortunately, his father spoke first and saved him the decision. "Your sister said don't forget to brush your teeth."

T'Challa laughed aloud, and all his stress left him, if only for a moment. That was just like Shuri. They argued and kidded each other just like Zeke and Sheila did.

"Well," T'Challa said, "I will, as long as she stays out of my room!"

"Message delivered," the Black Panther replied.

There was a moment of silence.

T'Challa faltered a moment, the smallest sign of distress, but it was enough for his father to pick up on. The Black Panther tilted his head in concern. "Is everything okay, son?"

"Yes," T'Challa said quickly. "Think I still have a little jet lag."

"You should be feeling fine by now. You've been there a while. Tell me, is there anything I should know?"

T'Challa was torn and hoped his internal struggle wasn't clear on his face. He didn't want to keep things from his father, but he once again thought of his duty to his friends. He didn't want them to face Achebe alone.

If I tell him about Achebe, what will he say? What will he do? Put me on a plane back home? Send help?

No. It's up to me. I have to make my own decisions. I won't abandon my friends. Not now. Not ever.

The Black Panther raised his dark eyebrows.

"I'm fine, Father," T'Challa finally said. "Really."

"The last thing you need is to get involved in another dangerous situation," his father warned him. "Like before. Promise me you'll be careful while you're there, T'Challa."

"I will," T'Challa promised him.

"My king," T'Challa heard in the background, a sign that the Black Panther was needed elsewhere. His father turned away from the screen, his face in profile.

"Duty calls, son," he said, turning back. "Best be going. Stay in touch."

The image flashed out with a blink.

T'Challa fingered a bead on his bracelet. A bird danced around in the high branches of the magnolia tree above him, whistling its nightly song. The internal struggle still volleyed back and forth in his head.

I should have said something.

No.

I can handle this.

I did it before and I can do it again.

He began to walk back over to join Zeke and Sheila.

I won't leave my friends—or this town—in danger. I will be a different type of leader. One who always—

"Talking to yourself?" Zeke said, interrupting T'Challa's thoughts.

"No," T'Challa said. "It was my father. Just checking in."

Zeke feigned a sad face, turning down his bottom lip. "Wish you had told us. We could've said hi."

T'Challa chuckled. "He was pretty busy, so . . ."

"T'Challa," Sheila said, her voice suddenly ominous. "Zeke."

They both turned to Sheila.

Sheila swallowed and looked to her tablet. "I just discovered something. Something you both need to see."

T'Challa sat down in one of the lawn chairs. He didn't know how many more surprises he could take, and steadied his mind for another.

"Remember when Zeke suggested we record Achebe's speech?" she asked.

Zeke and T'Challa both nodded.

"Well," Sheila continued, "it was a good idea. I wrote out what Achebe said the other night so I could study it more closely. There's a . . . subliminal message."

"Subliminal?" Zeke asked.

"Yeah," Sheila replied. "I didn't look at the video again while I was listening to it—didn't want to get hypnotized or anything—so I just wrote down the words. I knew there was something odd about the way he was speaking. He put an emphasis on the words he wanted people to *really* hear!"

Sheila turned the tablet so he and Zeke could both see. The screen glowed in the near dark.

"Read the words in bold," Sheila said.

T'Challa and Zeke huddled together and read the page to themselves:

*Now, **I** believe there is a great **need** in the world today.*
*A need for those **willing** to stand up.*
*That is the purpose of Rising **Souls**.*
The world today is crying out.
There are so many lost souls out there . . .
*people who need a cause, something **to devote their lives to**.*
I am here to deliver you.
***A higher cause** awaits.*
Come with me . . . listen.
I will call on you.
Wait for my voice. . . .
Solstitium
Solstitium.

T'Challa went numb. "'I need willing souls . . .'" he said.

"'To devote their lives to a higher cause,'" Zeke finished. "That is straight-up crazy! Who would say that?"

"Someone who's looking for souls," Sheila said.

There was a moment of silence.

"Good work, Sheila," T'Challa finally said. "You too, Zeke, for thinking of recording it."

"There was that white flash at the beginning," Zeke said. "Remember? Maybe that was part of it. And the weird metronome thing and the wavy red curtain."

"They all worked together to create an hypnotic effect," Sheila finished.

T'Challa sat back down and waved a hand through his hair. "Sheila, when did you say the solstice was?"

Sheila took her phone from her pocket. Her thumbs tapped furiously. "Four days from now. June twentieth." She paused. "It says that the summer solstice is the longest day of the year and also the shortest night. It's a time of"—she looked up from her phone—"rebirth."

T'Challa swallowed.

"Rebirth," Zeke repeated. "Like getting a new soul."

"We don't have a lot of time left," T'Challa said. "Whatever Achebe's doing is happening soon."

T'Challa sat back in his chair.

What was Achebe's plan?

How many people heard the message?

How many would heed it?

And, more importantly, what was Achebe going to do when they answered his call?

CHAPTER TWENTY-ONE

T'Challa got up a little before sunrise and headed to the backyard. He wanted some time alone before everyone was awake. He needed to think before he was met with any more startling revelations. What other strange events could the day hold?

He walked through the kitchen and then out into the backyard. The humidity was already high, and he felt the muggy air stir around him. He took a seat in one of the lawn chairs and put his feet up on a little bench. The pile of red sand was still on the concrete patio slab. *Where the sand runs like blood. Could the cave really be the place?*

Birds chirped and danced in the trees, hopping from branch to branch. The sun was a sliver of orange in the morning sky. He took a deep breath. The scent of Miss Rose's flowers filled his nostrils. But it was a fleeting moment.

I need willing souls to devote their lives to a higher cause.

He ran through all the mysterious phrases he had heard over the past several days, trying to see how they connected:

A room without books is like a body without a soul.

Young Prince. We will meet where the sand runs like blood.

Open me. Turn the page.

The Darkhold *is calling, Young Panther. Are you worthy?*

None of it fit together. They were all separate phrases that had their own meaning, but what did they mean all together?

The sun rose, spreading yellow light among the treetops. T'Challa felt its warm rays on his skin. He was reminded of home once again.

Home.

Father.

I should talk to him again. He probably knows Achebe, or has at least heard of him.

T'Challa battled within himself, his mind racing, not staying on one subject long enough to get any real insight.

Solstitium. Three days from now.

The sliding door creaked open.

"Whew," Sheila said. "Gave me a fright."

T'Challa snapped out of his thoughts.

"Me and Zeke are downstairs. Neither of us could sleep. We didn't see you and, well . . ."

"I'm safe and sound," T'Challa said. "Just thinking."

Sheila slid the door closed and sat down in another chair. She looked out at the morning sun, a cup of tea in hand.

"Some vacation, huh?" she asked.

T'Challa almost laughed. "Maybe one day we can just have a *normal* vacation."

"Yes," Sheila said. "Me and Zeke can come to Wakanda, and you can show us around."

"I wish," T'Challa said.

"So how does it work?" Sheila asked. "Who can actually visit Wakanda?

T'Challa knew the answer, and he was embarrassed to think that he couldn't tell her, even though she was one of his closest friends. He knew state secrets, and he had to keep them private.

"No one, really," he said.

"What do you mean?"

T'Challa lifted his feet from the bench. "Well, people do come to Wakanda, ambassadors from other countries, but they only see what we *want* them to see. . . ."

"Lord above!" a voice cried out.

"Gramma!" Sheila shouted as she and T'Challa launched out of their chairs.

T'Challa flung the sliding door open so quickly, it shattered as it hit the other end.

They raced inside, tripping over each other as they did so.

Miss Rose sat still on the couch, her eyes glued to the TV. Zeke stood frozen by her side, a bowl of cereal in his hands.

Sheila scurried to her side. "Gramma! What's wrong? What happened?"

But she didn't have to answer, as the announcer on the TV did all the talking:

"That's right, Jim. Sad news to report on WBEA Live. *This morning, several Beaumont residents have reported friends and family members missing. We're still waiting for an official count from police, but our early reports indicate that as many as . . . twenty people have just . . . disappeared. Police are urging citizens to shelter in place for the moment. We now go live to WBEA'S Connie Cline with the latest."*

T'Challa stood motionless.

"No," Sheila whispered. "It can't be."

"Lord above," Miss Rose said again. "What in the world is happening?"

T'Challa cast a sidelong glance at his friends.

They knew what was happening.

It was Achebe.

CHAPTER TWENTY-TWO

The town immediately went into high alert, and police cars patrolled the streets at all hours. Missing-person flyers started appearing everywhere: taped to street lamps and telephone poles, slipped under doors, and left on car windshields.

T'Challa and his friends were certain of one thing: The missing people were the ones who had listened to Achebe's video.

Miss Rose wouldn't let them stray far, and the next day was spent at Base Camp, trying to figure things out. The summer solstice was only two days away, and they needed answers.

"Look," Zeke said, scrolling through his laptop. "There's

going to be a candlelight vigil on the Town Green tomorrow for the missing people."

"I thought the police said to shelter in place," T'Challa said.

"No one tells people in Alabama what to do," Sheila pointed out. "We have to go. Sometimes criminals like to blend in and watch the consequences of their own crimes."

"Maybe Achebe will even be there," Zeke said, and then seemed to realize just how frightful that would be.

T'Challa felt fear as well.

But he wasn't going to let it win.

T'Challa felt trapped the rest of the day, but there was nothing they could do under the watchful eye of Miss Rose. Instead, they went over the same clues and information they had previously.

"We're not getting anywhere," T'Challa said.

"And we can't even get out of this house, either," Zeke complained, who seemed to be so out of sync, he wasn't even eating snacks.

"We just have to wait, then," Sheila said.

And wait they did, as hard as it was.

Tomorrow, T'Challa thought as he tried to fall asleep that night. *Tomorrow is the vigil. We have to get more answers. Or head straight to the caves.*

As he drifted in and out of sleep, T'Challa thought about his trip and what he had fallen into. Days of sightseeing and good food had turned into a nightmare. How could so many people just up and disappear? How did Achebe have such power?

It was supernatural. It had to be.

He slipped back into sleep with Achebe's words ringing in his ears:

I need willing souls . . .

Night was falling as they left the house and walked to the Town Green the next evening. T'Challa's stomach fluttered all day, and as much as he and his friends wanted to rush, Miss Rose led the way slowly, her face set and determined. "Shelter in place my . . . foot. We have to show support for Mr. McGuire and the others."

T'Challa saw the fierceness in Miss Rose's eyes and knew she was not one to tangle with.

Other Beaumont citizens were out as well, quietly walking to the vigil. MISSING signs stood out on lampposts and telephone poles. Men, women, and children, all gone. Vanished. There didn't seem to be any pattern, T'Challa realized. They came from all walks of life. Their portraits showed them smiling or laughing; at work or play; with family, pets, and friends. "We have to help them," T'Challa whispered. "We have to."

T'Challa saw the candles before he saw the people. They lined the Town Green on every side, small flames of hope to brighten the dark. One large poster board displayed the faces of the missing, and family members caressed the photographs, as if somehow their loved ones could feel how much they were missed. T'Challa thought his heart would break just looking at it.

The night was warm, and fireflies winked and floated on the night air. Uniformed police officers were peppered throughout the crowd. Groups sat on blankets or in lawn chairs, holding candles and talking quietly. An elderly woman handed out glasses of cold drinks while a young girl strummed a tune on a guitar. If not for the grim occasion, it would have been a pleasant and happy gathering.

"Be on the lookout," T'Challa warned his friends.

"For what?" Zeke asked.

T'Challa looked left, then right. "Anything."

Miss Rose accepted a lawn chair from a man and took a seat. T'Challa and his friends stood by themselves.

A Black man with a salt-and-pepper beard called the crowd to attention. He was tall, with a bald head and wire-frame glasses. "If I can have your attention for a moment," he said, tapping a microphone. "Attention, please."

The murmuring ceased.

The man coughed slightly and then began speaking. "Many of you here know me, but for those of you who don't, my name is Henry Toodle, and I'm the mayor of Beaumont."

Several people in the crowd applauded lightly.

"I'm happy to see you all here tonight, in this great show of support for our loved ones who have gone missing."

T'Challa peered around as the man spoke. He felt something in the air, some kind of tension, but he couldn't quite put his finger on it.

"We're joined here by the local Beaumont police," Mr. Toodle went on, "and the FBI is also lending their expertise. . . ."

The mayor paused and rubbed his brow, then took out a white handkerchief and dabbed his face. He looked out at the audience. "I . . . um . . . I have . . . a message."

T'Challa tensed.

Mr. Toodle's voice was different from a moment ago—slower and more halting.

"Something's wrong," T'Challa whispered.

"Yes," Mr. Toodle went on. "I have . . . a message."

The mayor swallowed loudly, and it was picked up by the microphone. It was as if he were struggling to regain his own thoughts and actions, something T'Challa had seen only once before:

With Mika.

Mayor Toodle coughed, and then swallowed loudly again, as if he had something stuck in his throat. "The message says: *The Dark—The Darkhold* is waiting, Young Panther. . . ."

T'Challa froze.

"No," Sheila whispered.

"What the—?" Zeke said.

A babble of confused murmuring rippled through the Town Green.

Mayor Toodle looked out at the assembled citizens, and even though he was several feet away, T'Challa saw the red flush in his eyes.

"Are you . . ." the mayor went on, his eyes searching. "Are you worthy?"

"Something's happened to him," Sheila whispered. "Somehow, Achebe got to him!"

The mayor suddenly stood up straight and shook his head, as if awakening from a dream. "Hello?" he said, his voice wavering. "Had a little migraine there. I was . . . Where was I?"

"What in the world is happening in this town?" Miss Rose whispered.

T'Challa scanned the crowd, looking for anything unusual. Was Achebe here, hidden away and taunting them? Why was he doing this to the mayor?

There were too many questions. Too much to think about. He clenched and unclenched his fists as a surge of adrenaline began to run through his body.

Tomorrow, on the solstitium, he would have answers.

CHAPTER TWENTY-THREE

Back home, the trio retired to Base Camp. Miss Rose went to bed after a cup of tea, still shocked and confused by the mayor's strange behavior.

"I say we sneak out and go to the cave tonight," Sheila demanded. "Why are we waiting on Achebe? If we go now, we might take him by surprise!"

"If he's even *in* the cave," Zeke said. "We're still assuming it's the place where the sand runs like blood."

T'Challa pondered Sheila's suggestion. "I don't know, guys. It's like he's playing some kind of game and we have to obey the rules if we're to stand a chance of defeating him.

He mentioned solstitium for a reason. I say we wait till the light of day to head out."

Zeke looked relieved, to T'Challa's mind.

"How do we get out?" Zeke asked. "Tomorrow, I mean."

"That's easy," Sheila replied. "Every Saturday, Gramma goes out to eat with Mrs. McGuire and some of her other friends. They're all retired. She calls them the Breakfast Bunch."

"Well," T'Challa said, "if she doesn't go, we're going to have to find a way out without getting her suspicious."

They all sat in silence for a long moment. Sheila yawned, followed by Zeke.

"Let's get some sleep," T'Challa said. "Tommorow's going to be . . ."

He paused. Doubt and fear was plain as day on his friends' faces.

He never finished the sentence.

T'Challa lay in bed. He remembered walking home from the vigil just a short while ago. For every house they passed, he wondered if its inhabitants were missing a loved one and racked with grief and consoling each other. At least twenty people were gone, according to the news report. *Twenty,* he thought as he drifted off to sleep. *Twenty souls . . .*

The light that shone in through the window the next morning was a bright spot in what T'Challa knew would be a dark day.

He roused himself from sleep and noticed Zeke wasn't in the room. For a fleeting moment he thought that maybe his friend had been kidnapped again, and was relieved when he saw him in the kitchen.

"Well," T'Challa said quietly as he entered the kitchen. "Is Miss Rose here?"

"No," Sheila said. "She left early to join her friends for breakfast."

T'Challa relaxed his shoulders, letting go of the tension. "Did she say anything? Like, don't go anywhere?"

"She did," Sheila replied. "But then I asked her why *she* could go out and we couldn't."

"That stumped her," Zeke said.

"I told her we would be careful if we did. Safety in numbers and all that, and she seemed to buy it."

"Good," T'Challa said.

But how long will we be gone? he wondered.

His stomach fluttered. This was it. They were going to the cave expecting danger. There was no other way. They had to get *The Darkhold*, and then . . .

"No," Sheila whispered, looking at her tablet. "No, no, no!"

T'Challa jumped, looking for an intruder or enemy.

But there wasn't one.

It was Sheila, standing transfixed with her tablet in her hands.

"What is it?" T'Challa asked, moving closer.

Sheila turned the tablet so they could all see:

MISSING
MIKA BELLOUARD

Beaumont Police are asking for information on the disappearance of Mika Bellouard, a sixteen-year-old summer employee of McGuire's Antique Emporium. Bellouard marks the twenty-first person reported missing in recent days. Her employer, notable Beaumont citizen Charles McGuire, was one of the first to be reported missing. Anyone with information on Ms. Bellouard's disappearance or any other's is urged to call Beaumont Police.

T'Challa opened his mouth to speak, but no words came. He felt a swirling range of emotions: Fear. Anger. Sadness. "Mika," he whispered. He saw her bright smile in his mind's eye. *She has to be okay,* he thought. *She has to be.*

"There's no time to waste," Sheila said, taking charge and bringing T'Challa back to the moment. She set the tablet on the table and clapped her hands together. "C'mon, Zeke! Put down that toast! Get packed. We need to get to that cave . . . now!"

▲▲▲

T'Challa raced to his room, taking the stairs two at a time. He opened his black leather bag and removed a few items to reveal the panther suit. "Didn't think I'd need you," he said aloud, and ran his fingers along the fabric. He recalled the last time he had put on the suit. It was in Chicago. A different city and a different threat. He exhaled and zipped up the bag, then slung it over his shoulder and headed downstairs.

Sheila and Zeke carried backpacks with water and proper flashlights along with a random assortment of supplies: a lighter, a compass, and several packs of trail mix, which Zeke insisted on bringing.

"T'Challa?" Sheila said. "You ready?"

T'Challa exhaled a breath. "I'm ready," he said, and then: "Guys. Listen."

Zeke and Sheila paused.

T'Challa looked at both of them for a moment and held their gazes. "Okay. We're walking into the unknown. We have to be careful."

"Of course," Zeke said.

"What I'm saying is," T'Challa continued, "if we run into trouble, let me sort it out. I don't want you guys getting hurt. If I say run, I want you to *run*. Okay?"

Zeke and Sheila both stared.

"T'Challa," Sheila said. "You should know by now, after last time, we're in this together. We'd never abandon you in the middle of danger. If it gets really bad, we'll *all* hightail it out of there. Right, Zeke?"

Zeke crossed his arms over his chest. "Wakanda forever," he said.

T'Challa smiled, realizing he had two of the best friends one could ever hope for.

"Let's do this," Zeke said.

T'Challa looked at his friend. He was proud of him. Even after what Zeke had gone through, he was still willing to walk into the unknown. T'Challa promised himself once again to keep him safe.

Outside, T'Challa looked up and studied the sun. Summer solstice. Solstitium. A time of rebirth. He thought of his ancestors, the five tribes of Wakanda. They had gazed upon the same sun thousands of years ago. "Give me strength, ancestors," he said quietly. "Bast protect me."

The sun was blazing by the time they reached Vulcan Park, which was already full of early-morning tourists. They headed toward the mountain range immediately. Zeke shook his head as they walked.

"What is it?" T'Challa asked.

"I can't remember anything," Zeke said, frustrated. "I mean, how did I even get out here?"

"Hopefully we'll get answers," Sheila said.

Unfortunately, T'Challa thought, her optimism didn't sound too convincing.

Zeke hitched his pack up on his shoulders. He groaned. "Hey, Sheila. You didn't say we'd be going on another adventure when you invited us to Alabama."

Sheila gave a snort. "Uh, it wasn't my idea."

"What do you mean?" Zeke asked.

"Just what I said. Weren't you the first one to bring up a summer vacation, since you knew my gramma was here?"

"Nope," Zeke said.

Sheila wiped sweat from her brow. She paused and halted their march. "Seriously? Alabama wasn't my idea. Was it yours, T'Challa?"

T'Challa felt a buzz of apprehension circle around them.

"No," he said. "I remember video calls, but I don't remember who originally suggested the trip."

"This *is* weird," Zeke said.

The cry of a hawk sounded overhead. T'Challa could see the cave entrance now, not too far ahead. A heat haze danced around the opening.

"So," T'Challa said, "we're all saying that none of us came up with the idea of coming here?"

"If we didn't," Zeke said cautiously, "who did?"

They all knew the answer, but none of them spoke it aloud.

"Dreams," T'Challa said. "We know Achebe has been in my dreams. So he's been in yours, too."

"I don't remember any Achebe dreams, though," Sheila countered.

"Me either," Zeke said.

T'Challa shook his head. "Maybe he wanted it that way. Maybe he's only in my dreams now to get me to . . ."

"To what?" Sheila asked.

"That's just it," T'Challa replied. "I don't know what he wants."

T'Challa paused in his thinking. There was one thing he never considered. With all the talk of how evil *The Darkhold* was, he never thought about what they would do once they got it. *If* they got it. How could they destroy it? The research said it was written on indestructible parchment. On that somber note, they picked up their pace again and kept moving.

A few minutes later, they had arrived at the entrance to the cave. Cool air drifted out. T'Challa turned to his friends and gave them both a weak smile. "Stay on your guard."

Daylight turned to deepest night as they entered the cave. T'Challa used a Kimoyo bead for light. Zeke and Sheila aimed their flashlights along the cave floor.

"Cold in here," Zeke said.

"Forgot to bring sweaters," Sheila put in.

"Nothing to do for it now," T'Challa said.

They walked in silence for a while, and T'Challa thought about what Sheila had said, that she wasn't the one to plan the trip. He didn't want to imagine the worst—that Achebe had lured them all to Alabama somehow—but he had to consider it. How else could it have happened?

T'Challa kept his eyes and ears peeled for any sudden movements. He brought Sheila and Zeke to a halt. Achebe was dangerous, there was no doubt of that. He needed to protect himself and his friends, and there was only one way to do it.

"Just a minute," he said.

He slung the bag off his shoulder and set it on the damp ground.

Sheila screwed up her face. "You're gonna get mud all over that nice bag."

T'Challa unzipped the bag.

"T," Zeke inquired, "what are you doing?"

Inside the bag, folded into a perfect square, was a piece of fabric. T'Challa drew it out with an air of reverence.

Zeke's eyes lit up.

"Wow," Sheila said, shining her flashlight up and down the suit. "Is that the same one as before?"

T'Challa let the fabric unfold, and it cascaded to his feet like a wave of black silk. "Yes, but it's lighter. My sister, Shuri, suggested some adjustments."

"Shuri?" Zeke said, pushing his glasses back up on his nose. "Isn't she just a little kid?"

T'Challa smiled. "Well, if little kids understand the concept of string theory and know how to write code, then yeah, she's a kid."

"Wow," Zeke said. "She sounds like a mini Sheila."

"Hopefully you can meet her one day. I know she'd love you, Sheila."

Sheila smiled. "I'd be happy to meet Princess Shuri."

"Give me a second," T'Challa said as he darted a few

short steps away to a shadowy corner. T'Challa handled the suit carefully, like it was a newborn kitten or an egg that could easily crack. He slipped out of his clothes and placed them in the bag to be picked up later. *I hope,* he suddenly thought.

T'Challa put on the suit. He felt as if he had just slid into a bottle of luxurious black ink. What looked like glittering stars winked within the Vibranium-mesh fabric. It was stronger than chain mail and a fraction of its weight. It felt good to wear it again, he realized. He remembered the first time he had put it on. It fit his form snugly but also gave him enough room to move freely.

He didn't have a mask, like his father's suit, but what he did have was thousands of interlaced Vibranium modules embedded in the fabric, which, once in contact with skin, gave its wearer extra protection and a heightened sense of awareness. T'Challa stretched his neck in a circle and bounced on his toes a few times. He punched the air and ran in place for twenty seconds. The nanites monitored his pulse, heart rate, and breathing. He felt as if he could sprint a hundred miles. Any blow or damage he took while wearing the suit would be absorbed into the material and redirected as kinetic energy back at an opponent.

He let out a breath. "Here goes," he said.

CHAPTER TWENTY-FOUR

"Ah, yeah!" Zeke drawled.

T'Challa felt self-conscious in his suit for the briefest of moments, but the feeling quickly faded.

"Looks great," Sheila said.

"I'm only wearing this in case we run into trouble," T'Challa told them. "This isn't for fun."

"Wish I had a suit," Zeke complained.

If their situation wasn't so dire, T'Challa would have laughed. He had a sudden memory of Zeke from last year, when he wore a homemade costume and called himself Red Lightning when they were on their mission. This time

Zeke's outfit was different, T'Challa noticed. His T-shirt read: BLACK NERDS UNITE.

"Follow me," T'Challa said.

T'Challa led the way, every one of his senses on high alert. His vision, hearing, even the damp, musty smell of the cave was heightened. *I have to find them,* he thought. *Mr. McGuire and Mika. All of them. I have to.*

"You know how to remember the difference between stalactites and stalagmites?" Zeke asked, his voice echoing. He pointed to a long stalactite, formed into a glittering point.

"No," said Sheila, who surely did know. "Please enlighten us."

"Well," Zeke said, "the word stalactite has a letter *c*, so remember *c* for *ceiling*. And stalagmite has a *g*, so that stands for *ground*."

"Fascinating," Sheila said.

T'Challa's footsteps were quiet, absorbed by the ground under his feet. A clicking sound alerted his sensors. "What was that?" he asked, pausing.

"What was what?" Zeke replied, looking around nervously.

"A clicking sound," T'Challa said. "It was kind of high-pitched."

"I didn't hear anything," Zeke said.

"Must be the suit," T'Challa pointed out, "picking up on the slightest noises."

Sheila aimed her flashlight up at the hidden corners. "There's the culprit," she said.

T'Challa looked up.

"It's a flock of bats!" Zeke cried.

"Shh!" Sheila whisper-shouted. "It's a cauldron, also called a colony. When they're in flight, they're referred to as a cloud."

"Hmpf," Zeke said, impressed. "A cloud of bats. I might use that for a comic book idea one day."

"Bats use high-frequency sound for communication," Sheila went on. "Humans usually can't hear it."

"Unless you're the freaking Black Panther," Zeke said, a little too loudly.

"I'm not the Black Panther *yet*," T'Challa corrected him. "That's my father. One day, I may be able to wear the mantle."

"*Mantle*," Zeke repeated. "Why do they call it a mantle and not a cloak?"

T'Challa paused. "That's a good question, Zeke. I would imagine that long ago, the Black Panthers of old wore the mantle. The same one is passed down from generation to generation. Maybe the word *mantle* was more popular than the word *cloak* back then. I don't know."

"Interesting," Sheila said.

T'Challa took note of Zeke's light mood. Maybe it was all a defense against fear, nervous energy that had to be directed somewhere other than the foreboding situation they found themselves in.

"Well," Zeke said apprehensively, "better watch out, anyway. Don't want to get bitten."

"They're fine," Sheila said. "Bats don't attack people."

"Oh yeah?" Zeke countered. "Ever seen that movie *Zombie Bats*?"

Sheila aimed her flashlight at Zeke, who shaded his eyes with his hand. "Right. That's a movie. There is no classification for zombie bats."

"Okay," T'Challa said. "That's enough—"

What sounded like a muffled laugh echoed around them.

T'Challa immediately went into a defensive stance. He peered around, searching the dark cave. Zeke and Sheila both stood as still as statues.

"It came from over here," T'Challa said, pointing to their right. "C'mon. Follow me."

They paused. Zeke looked at T'Challa. "Let me get this straight. We're walking *into* the crazy laughter?"

"That's what we came here for, Zeke," T'Challa answered. "We've *already* walked into it."

"Right," Sheila said. "Too late to turn back now."

Zeke and Sheila fell in behind T'Challa as he once more led the way. The path became so narrow, they had to walk single file—T'Challa in the front and Sheila in the rear. There was barely enough room to stretch one's arms out to either side without touching the damp walls.

"Does any of this look familiar, Zeke?" T'Challa asked, his voice echoing.

"Nope. Not at all."

"Ouch!" Sheila cried, furiously waving her hand in front of her face.

T'Challa turned around quickly, ready to lash out.

"I'm okay," Sheila said. "Felt like something was in my hair."

"Zombie bat," Zeke said.

T'Challa turned back around and continued walking. He felt safe in the suit, and wished his friends had some sort of protection as well. *That would be me,* he suddenly realized. He was their protector. He had to keep them safe. That's what super heroes did.

As they continued on, all T'Challa heard was his friends' footsteps and the constant drip of water from the cave roof.

"T'Challa?" Zeke suddenly called. "Where'd you go?"

"Right here," T'Challa said, turning around.

Zeke shook his head. "Wow. You were only a few steps in front of us and I couldn't see you!"

"It's the suit," T'Challa said. "A feature called Stealth helps me blend into any environment."

"Incredible," Sheila said.

After a few more minutes, a lighter shade of black loomed ahead of them. "Something's up here," T'Challa whispered.

Sure enough, the tunnel expanded out to a cavernous area with a fine reddish dirt and a few large boulders. The remains of several rusted mine carts were shoved against one wall and scattered along the floor, their parts reminiscent of some forgotten mechanical beast.

T'Challa stepped carefully around the broken machinery.

He froze.

"Guys," he said.

Zeke and Sheila caught up with him.

"This . . . dirt," he said, pointing. "It's red."

"It's finer," Sheila said. "More like sand now."

" 'Where the sand runs like blood,' " T'Challa whispered.

Sheila looked at her friend, his form barely visible in the dark. "So this is it. The place where Achebe said he would meet you."

T'Challa looked around the cave, searching, his eyes taking in every corner. "Well," he boasted, "let him come, then."

Zeke shot him an approving grin. "Why here, though?" he asked. "What's so special about this place?"

But he didn't get an answer.

"What's that?" Sheila said.

Small flickering lights waved in an unfelt breeze several feet in front of them. At first, T'Challa thought they were fireflies, but as they drew closer, he saw what they really were: thick white candles stuck into mounds of reddish dirt. They formed a circle around a black pedestal about four feet tall. And something sat atop it.

"I've seen this before," T'Challa whispered. "In my dreams."

Open me, he heard inside his head. *Turn the page.*

"It's *The Darkhold,*" T'Challa said, his voice void of emotion.

Zeke and Sheila exchanged a cautious glance.

T'Challa felt himself being drawn forward, a pull he couldn't seem to resist.

"T'Challa," Sheila said, a note of fear in her usually confident voice. "What are you doing?"

Come, the voice called in T'Challa's head. *Open me. Turn the page.*

Everything seemed to fall away at that moment for T'Challa—the cave, his friends, everything. The book was calling him. He had to answer it.

He felt his insides churning, an urge like he had never experienced before, a magnet drawing him closer and closer. . . .

He took another step forward.

And another.

"T'Challa!" Zeke shouted. "Don't touch it!"

But he did.

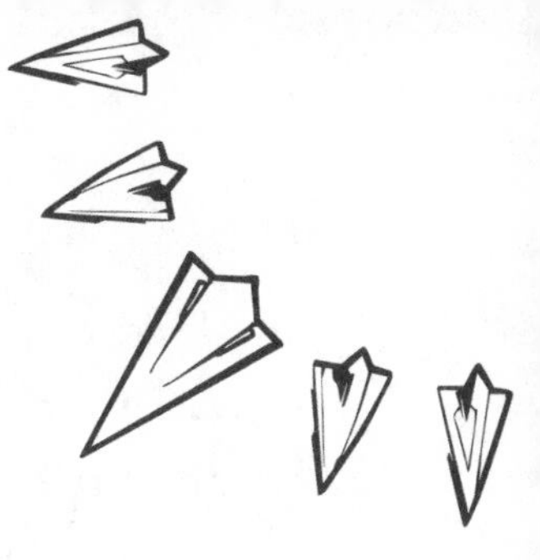

CHAPTER TWENTY-FIVE

T'Challa stood in front of the pedestal and looked down at the book. Just like in his dream, the cover showed faces in various forms of agony—silent screams of the doomed.

Open me. Turn the page.

Slowly, as if he were about to touch a poisonous snake, T'Challa reached out with his left hand. The tormented faces writhed and twisted, as if trying to break free.

"T'Challa," Zeke whispered, his voice a warning.

T'Challa touched the cover.

He waited for something to happen—lightning bolts crashing down from the ceiling, the ground opening up, or any kind of catastrophe, but all was silent, except for the blood rushing in his temples. Zeke and Sheila sighed a breath of relief and crept up beside him.

The book was iron gray and cold to the touch—a cold so deep, it was almost hot. The symbols Mika had drawn were clearly etched in the surface: star, moon, and broken chain. But now T'Challa saw another symbol, one that could only be described as an insect with numerous legs. Words were burned into the surface, the letters red and fiery. T'Challa took a closer look. "It's in Xhosa," he said, astonished. "The words are in my country's language!"

Sheila looked over T'Challa's shoulder. She cocked her head. "No it's not. What are you talking about? It's English."

"Yeah," Zeke said. "I see English, too."

T'Challa ran his finger along the cover. The words were clearly written in Xhosa. "'Abandon all hope, ye who enter here,'" he read.

"Great," Zeke said. "Sounds normal."

"It's from the *Divine Comedy*," Sheila explained. "'Inferno.' Lasciate ogni speranza, voi ch'entrate."

"Show-off," Zeke said. "How can it be in different languages?"

"Because the book shows its reader what they want to see," a voice called out.

And it wasn't one of them.

The trio spun around.

Achebe's shadow appeared before he did, a looming figure that spread along the cave wall like a bolt of black fabric. But he didn't look like an acrobat anymore. He was dressed in a long red robe bordered with gold trim, and he held something in his hand, but T'Challa couldn't see what it was. Achebe stopped about thirty feet in front of them.

"Where is he?" Sheila challenged him. "Where's Mr. McGuire?"

"And Mika and the others," Zeke said.

Achebe's Cheshire Cat grin landed on Zeke. "Ah, there you are. Zeke, isn't it? I knew you would be back."

T'Challa cocked his head, curious.

"So you *did* bring me here," Zeke said. "Why? Why'd you let me get away?"

"How else could I be guaranteed you'd return?" Achebe said smugly. "With your . . . princely friend, of course."

"Where are they?" T'Challa said, trying his best to concentrate and not get sucked into Achebe's game. "What did you do with them?"

Achebe raised his left hand and began to speak. And that's when T'Challa saw what it was that he held. It was a hand puppet in Achebe's likeness, wearing the same red-and-gold robe. The similarities, even down to Achebe's mad grin, were startling. "Did you hear that, Daki?" Achebe said. "He wants to know where my souls are."

Daki, T'Challa thought. *Zeke said something about someone named Daki. A puppet?*

T'Challa narrowed his eyes and studied Achebe and the weird puppet. He recalled the research they had done a while back. It said Achebe was smart and gifted, but his personality was tinged with madness.

Achebe's gaze went back to T'Challa. "I knew you would come. Just like your father, the mighty Black Panther. Just can't help getting involved, can you? Did he ever tell you I almost ousted him in a coup?"

T'Challa didn't answer, but Zeke had his own opinion to share. "Yeah, right. He'd kick your—"

"It's true," Achebe cut him off. "I'm surprised you don't know more about your country's history, T'Challa."

"Take his name out of your mouth," Sheila whispered.

T'Challa didn't have time for a history lesson. He'd have to look into that later. Right now, the threat was here, standing directly in front of him. He clenched his fists. He could actually hear the material stretching as he did so.

"How did you get into my head?" Zeke asked. "How did you get me to come here the other night?"

Achebe put on an innocent face, which looked difficult, considering his mad grin. "It wasn't just me. I had a little help."

As if on cue, a shape emerged from the surrounding darkness. T'Challa stood tense and ready. The figure came out into the open. His face was deathly pale, and an unruly shock of black hair stood up on his head.

"Please meet an acquaintance of mine," Achebe announced. "His name is Nightmare."

A sudden memory flooded T'Challa's brain.

He had seen this man before.

It was the same man he had bumped into after they left the arcade.

The same man who had made the sleeping gesture with his hands.

The Man in the Green Suit.

Nightmare dipped his head in greeting, as if this were all normal. For an instant, T'Challa thought he saw the man's eyes flash red.

"How, you ask," Nightmare began, "did I get inside your heads?" His eyes roamed over T'Challa and his friends. "You know what they say, don't you? Dreams are the windows to the soul."

T'Challa searched his memories for any mention of a creature called Nightmare but came up blank.

"It was very simple, really," Nightmare continued. "I am the King of Dreams, but I prefer the Midnight Leviathan. Has a good ring to it, don't you think? My power lies in the state of unawakening. The Land of Nod, as some call it."

Nightmare seemed to be relishing his moment, T'Challa saw, as if this were all some game, and not a matter of life and death.

"My friend here asked for a favor," Nightmare went on.

"Reach into the dreams of you three . . . children, and plant a suggestion. A suggestion to come to this place. Alabama." He held his hands up as if offering a prize, revealing several silver rings. "Very easy, really. Child's play."

Nightmare took a few steps forward. T'Challa backed up, knees bent, fists raised.

"No need to fight," Nightmare said. "I really abhor violence. I prefer torment through the power of dreams. Like the one where I told you to come here, where the sand runs like blood."

T'Challa shook his head. None of this was matching what he had thought.

"Yes, that was me," Nightmare went on, "putting that voice in your head."

Achebe shrugged his skinny shoulders and looked at T'Challa. "You didn't think it was *me*, did you?" he asked in mock sincerity. "I admit I am powerful, but not strong enough to plant voices in your head. My power lies in hypnosis and other . . . necessary skills."

"What about your face?" T'Challa said. "I saw your face in my dreams."

Nightmare actually did a little wave with his hand, directing the attention back to him. "All me," he said.

"The mayor," Sheila called out. "Mayor Toodle. Why did you . . . possess him?"

Nightmare looked to Achebe.

"Don't look at me," Achebe said.

Nightmare turned back to T'Challa and friends. "Toodle? What kind of name is that? No idea what you're talking about."

T'Challa tried to focus. *If it wasn't Achebe or Nightmare who possessed Mayor Toodle, then who was it? And what about Mika?*

"All my friend asked in return," Achebe said, "was that I use my powers to bring him a reward. A reward in the form of souls, people willing to devote themselves to a *higher* cause. Rising souls, you could call them."

Nightmare bowed dramatically.

"Catchy, huh?" Achebe said. "Rising Souls." He chuckled. "So obvious."

I need willing souls, T'Challa remembered, *to devote their lives to a higher cause.* He felt sick to his stomach. Achebe had been toying with them all this time.

"He will feast on their dreams," Achebe said softly, but his voice was full of menace. "Oh, what horrors await them!"

T'Challa shuddered. They were all brought here through dark magic. Nightmare had gotten into their heads. Now he stood here with Zeke and Sheila, facing two of the most dangerous foes imaginable.

"They weren't willing," T'Challa said in defiance. "They're innocent. Where are they?"

"No one is truly innocent," Achebe said. "You want to see your friends? Look. There they are. How could you have missed them? Don't you see their faces?"

T'Challa followed Achebe's finger. He was pointing to the book. *The Darkhold*.

"Show them," Achebe said in his Daki voice—a high-pitched shriek that sent a shiver down T'Challa's spine. "Yes, show them!"

Achebe turned the hand puppet to face him. "Don't be so dramatic! What did I tell you about butting in?"

Achebe actually turned himself around in a circle and used his Daki voice to reply. "Who are you to tell me what to do? I'm in charge here, fool!"

Achebe smacked the puppet with his free hand. "Shut up! Enough of your nonsense!"

Nightmare howled with laughter. T'Challa recoiled. It wasn't funny. It was disturbing.

"That's who he was arguing with when I was taken," Zeke whispered. "That weird puppet thing."

T'Challa turned back to the book, keeping an eye out for any sudden movements from Achebe. Zeke and Sheila followed his lead. T'Challa stared at the cover. He blinked.

It couldn't be.

"No," he said as the faces of Mr. McGuire and Mika appeared, along with others, their features distorted as if in a fun-house mirror. "No!"

But there was a new face there, too. One he would not have expected.

Sheila reached out a trembling hand. "Gramma?" she said, her voice quavering. "Gramma Rose!"

Sheila turned around, her face a mask of anger. "Let her out!" she shouted, drawing closer to Achebe. "Stop this!"

"Too late," Daki chirped. "Too late! Too late! Too late!"

Achebe dropped the puppet on the ground and bent down to gather a handful of the reddish dirt. "Where the sand runs like blood," he said. "Did you know, at one time, they called this land the Black Belt for its rich dark soil? But there is another element that brought me here. One of the only components on this earth ancient enough to be used in this ritual."

He let the red sand fall from his hands to land at the hem of his robe. "It is iron ore. Billions of years old, and a vital ingredient in the process of soul transference."

T'Challa swallowed hard.

Soul transference.

"I seek a divine connection between the human soul and the universe," Achebe went on. "That is all I ask."

T'Challa thought of the Vitruvian Man symbol and its reference to the soul.

"But it is not just any soul I seek," Achebe said. "I desire a powerful one. One strong enough to defeat the bravest of enemies, even the Black Panther himself."

Achebe began to move toward T'Challa, a serpent preparing to strike.

"But first," Achebe said, "there is something I need. Something very important."

T'Challa leaned forward, sensing an attack. "What?" he said.

"Your blood!" Achebe shouted, and leapt for T'Challa.

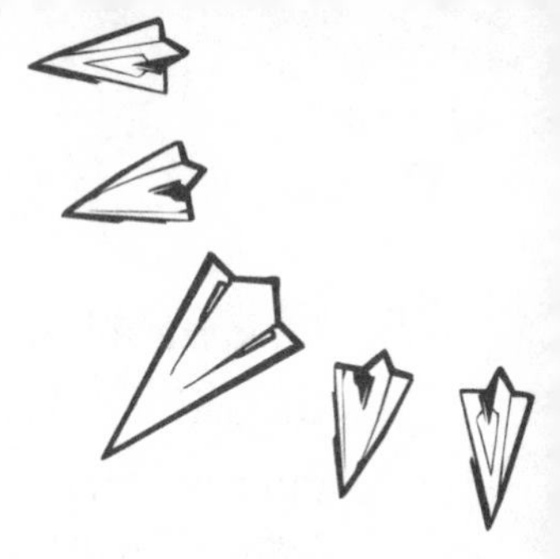

CHAPTER TWENTY-SIX

Achebe was like a ball of wiry rubber that had just been snapped. His long arms and legs seemed to be everywhere at once, and T'Challa struggled to land a blow.

Achebe grabbed T'Challa tight in a bear hug and drove his forehead right into his own. T'Challa fell back, stunned. He felt as if he had just been hit by a pile of bricks. Zeke and Sheila stood ready to help, looking for an opening, but the two figures were so locked together, they didn't get the chance. Nightmare stood in the shadows, boxing the air in a mock display.

T'Challa rose back up and lashed out with his right foot, spinning his body backward in a somersault kick. Achebe took the blow to the chin, but it didn't slow him down. Instead, he reached into his robe. T'Challa saw the silvery glint of steel flash in the dark. A long, curved dagger with gems embedded in the hilt was clutched in his right hand.

T'Challa clenched his left fist and then released it. Five Vibranium-tipped claws snapped out of his gloved knuckles, metal tips shining.

"One drop," Achebe said, tossing the blade from hand to hand. "One drop of royal blood isn't much to ask, is it?"

Blood? T'Challa thought, his mind racing. *What does he want with my blood?*

T'Challa maneuvered around Achebe, who suddenly went into his high-pitched Daki voice again. "One drop of blood will free my soul. Free my soul. Free my *SOUL*!"

Achebe leapt into the air as if he had springs in his boots. He came down hard, close to T'Challa, and swung the knife toward his midsection. T'Challa stepped back just in time. He actually felt the air from Achebe's swing. But he had missed. This time.

"Very good," Achebe said, dancing around T'Challa. "You are quick, but are you quick enough?"

Achebe scuttled up a pile of high rocks to his right, and then, using his acrobatic skill, tucked himself into a ball and launched himself toward T'Challa, landing on his feet at the last second.

T'Challa, surprised by how quickly his opponent moved,

stumbled back, but not before Achebe landed a blow on his jaw with his left hand.

T'Challa instinctively raised his hand to his mouth.

It came away slick with blood.

"Ah," Achebe whispered, rubbing his fingers together. "I have it now. The . . . blood!"

T'Challa's attention was drawn away as a blur flashed in the corner of his vision. It was Sheila.

Not hesitating in the slightest, she ran forward and reached out for the book.

"Those souls are mine!" Nightmare suddenly cried out, and raced to his prize.

But Sheila was faster.

She picked up the book.

"Aieee!" she screamed, dropping it on the ground. "It burns!"

Zeke ran to her side and tried to retrieve the book, but he suffered the same fate. He scrambled away, clutching his hand in pain.

T'Challa still struggled with Achebe as Nightmare spoke to Zeke and Sheila.

"Children," he said calmly, as if a battle between life and death wasn't unfolding just a few steps away. "You must show respect before touching such a valuable talisman."

He bent down and grasped the book. For a moment, nothing happened.

"See," Nightmare said. "Very simple."

But then . . .

A light flashed in Nightmare's eyes. Slowly, like water passing over a stone, a myriad of cracks began to form on his face. Zeke and Sheila took a step back.

Nightmare touched his cheek. "No," he said, dropping the book. "No!"

He screamed and then crumpled to the ground.

Achebe and T'Challa circled each other. *Why can't they touch the book?* T'Challa thought as madness and chaos swirled around him. *I did. Why can't they?*

T'Challa moved left, and so did Achebe. T'Challa then spun to his right, and Achebe followed suit. He was mimicking his movements. How could he anticipate T'Challa's moves so quickly? It was like looking at a mirror image of himself.

T'Challa feinted to his right and then quickly moved left. He swung, but Achebe ducked as T'Challa's claws scraped the rough cave wall, sending up a shower of sparks.

Achebe laughed and lunged, dagger held high.

But T'Challa crouched, spun, and took Achebe's legs out from under him.

Achebe hit the ground and sent up a cloud of red dust.

T'Challa dove onto the fallen figure and somehow was able to grab Achebe's wrist and twist, which made Achebe cry out in pain and drop the knife.

Achebe struggled against T'Challa's weight, trying to

break free with his wiry, spidery arms, but T'Challa pinned him in a wrestling move called the Cradle, with one arm around Achebe's neck and the other clutching his knee, but he wasn't sure what to do next. He eased up for one moment, about to give Achebe the chance to surrender, but that was a fatal mistake. All it took for Achebe to break T'Challa's grip on him was that one little ease-up of pressure. Achebe pushed him off and rose quickly.

Achebe used T'Challa's shock to his advantage and leapt toward the pedestal where *The Darkhold* was placed. "The blood!" he screamed like a banshee. "The royal blood!"

Zeke, seeing what was about to happen, rushed toward Achebe. "No!" he cried out. "Wakanda for—"

"Solstitium," Achebe whispered, and Zeke collapsed to the ground. Sheila rushed to his side.

Achebe raised his arms in the air and lunged toward *The Darkhold.*

As if in slow motion, T'Challa watched as Achebe's long outstretched arm smeared *The Darkhold*'s cover with his blood.

"No!" Sheila cried.

Immediately, a column of purple-and-red flame shot up from *The Darkhold* and singed the roof. Stalactites sizzled and melted, bringing down a torrent of rock and water. The iron ore around the pedestal ignited like a blast furnace and shot flames into the air. The ground trembled. T'Challa felt like the earth's tectonic plates were shifting under his feet.

"Aieeee!" Achebe screamed, but T'Challa didn't know if it was in joyful glee or pain.

Achebe held up both arms to the heavens. "Oh, Book of Sins!" he cried out. "Darkhold, Scroll of Chthon! Strip the young panther's soul from his body and release it to me!"

A red light began to appear along the spine of *The Darkhold*, as if a blade of fire were creeping along the edges. The cover flew open, and the pages ruffled as a terrible gust of sulfurous air filled the cave.

T'Challa felt as if his lungs would burst from the acrid smoke.

The flame that had erupted from the iron ore swirled and folded in on itself. Blue and purple and red and gold swirled like lava. The flame suddenly seemed to form itself into a figure, which quickly knit itself together.

T'Challa drew back at what he saw.

It stood as tall as a man, shrouded in a nimbus of flame and smoke. There was only the impression of a human face, but the mouth was visible, a deep chasm of fiery red.

"I am the Other," a voice spoke, and the cave walls seemed to shudder at the power of it.

The Other, T'Challa recalled with dread. *No. It can't be.*

He remembered what they had learned several days ago, during their research:

Chthon exists in a dimension not of this world, and cannot take physical form on Earth. Instead, he uses an entity called "the Other" to carry out his desires.

We're doomed, T'Challa realized. *This has all been for nothing. We will die here, in this cave.*

To T'Challa's amazement, Nightmare stirred on the ground and stood up on trembling legs, his face a map of wrinkles. He looked to T'Challa, then Achebe, and leapt for the book.

The Other raised a hand, and Nightmare rose in the air as if lifted by invisible wires. He struggled and screamed, arms and legs flailing. "He promised me!" Nightmare shouted. "Those souls are mine! I need their dreams to feed on!"

The demon twirled his fiery fist, and Nightmare turned upside down, head pointed to the ground as he continued to scream.

T'Challa watched it all unfold in front of him. He was winded, and his breath came in bursts.

"Speak!" the Other said to Achebe.

Achebe fell to his knees, trembling. "Yes, forgive me, great one. I . . . I didn't mean to disturb you."

The Other moved toward Achebe. "But you have, peasant. You have. Once *The Darkhold* is opened, I am called."

Achebe groveled on the ground, seemingly trying to gather his wits. "Yes. Yes. I see now. It is a long story, but I will shorten the tale for you, great one."

There was no way to get the book now, T'Challa knew. This was a demon from the darkest depths of the universe.

Achebe continued to writhe on his knees. He rubbed his hands together as he began to speak. "Great master," he started, "once, long ago, I was close to death, you see. But Mephisto, a sorcerer of great power, brought me back. I lost my soul in the bargain, for that was his price. To relinquish my soul to live again."

Mephisto, T'Challa thought. *Achebe was said to have sold his soul to an entity called Mephisto to gain power.*

A fiery halo around the Other's head flared brightly, hues of green and red filling the cave. Sheila had managed to rouse Zeke enough to move him away from the battle, and they were huddled against the cave wall, paralyzed by fear.

"There is a spell in *The Darkhold*," Achebe went on. "One that gives the summoner the power to take a human soul. It will only work if it is performed on the same day as when the spell was first written, long, long ago. And that day is today, Master, the day when the sun stands still, the solstitium." Achebe bowed his head. "That is what I desire."

Achebe raised his head. He pointed to T'Challa. "There he stands, the son of the mighty Black Panther. What better revenge than to take his son's soul for my very own?" Achebe lowered his head again in deference.

Revenge? T'Challa thought. *What is he talking about?*

There was another gust of flame from the fiery figure. T'Challa felt heat rippling along the air. A remaining stalactite melted and dripped to the cave floor.

The Other belched forth a gust of purple flame. "You dare summon Chthon! The Destroyer! For this!"

Achebe lowered his head even farther. "Yes, Master. Please!"

"Fool!" the Other hissed.

He raised his flame-streaked hand, and Achebe flew across the room as if he really were a puppet, slamming against the cave wall.

"Please!" Achebe begged, standing up slowly, his once-clean robe now mud-stained and slashed. "Grant me this one wish!"

"Yes," the Other said, "I will grant you your wish."

Achebe's mad eyes lit up.

"But not in this world," the Other promised him.

And then, as T'Challa watched, a red mist rose from *The Darkhold* and snaked its way along the floor. It slithered forward until it reached the hem of Achebe's robe. But it didn't stop there.

The Mad Acrobat looked down, horror dawning on his face as the mist rose higher and higher, working its way up his arm and to his shoulder.

"No!" he cried out in Daki's voice, a terrible wailing sound. "What is happening?"

"You are becoming . . ." the Other said, "one with *The Darkhold*, the Book of Shiatra."

The red vine continued to rise up Achebe's arm. There was a sudden jerk, and Achebe fell face-first onto the book. And then the book consumed him. The puppet, which had been tossed aside, crumpled and turned to ash. T'Challa heard a last faint cry from Achebe, and only silence followed.

Zeke moaned as the hypnosis relinquished its hold of him, and Sheila helped him wake up the rest of the way, their faces slick with sweat and their clothes in ruins.

The Other turned to Nightmare, still dangling in the air.

"No!" Nightmare pleaded. "Don't kill me! I only did what he asked!"

The Other raised both of his fiery arms in the air and *pushed*, sending Nightmare to the ground, where he collapsed. T'Challa thought the man was dead, but to his surprise, he scrambled up and ran for the cave exit.

The Other turned to face T'Challa.

T'Challa went into a defensive stance and snapped his claws, but he knew there was nothing he could do to defeat this creature. He was a demon god from another world.

The Other didn't speak for a long moment. His gaze turned to Zeke and Sheila, who turned away from his bright aura.

"The secrets of *The Darkhold* are not for one as . . . weak as Achebe," the Other said. "It needs another. One of strong mind and spirit. Come. Turn the page."

And that's when T'Challa realized it.

It wasn't Achebe who had been calling out to him. Achebe was a mortal man with earthbound skills. It was Chthon who had been tempting him. Chthon who had possessed Mika and Mayor Toodle. T'Challa swallowed hard.

"Don't listen to him, T'Challa!" Sheila warned him.

T'Challa looked to his friends and then back to the flaming demon.

"*The Darkhold* calls out to those who have the power to use it," the Other said. "It is stronger than *The Necronomicon*. Older than the *Oracles of Zoroaster.* All you've ever wished for, you can achieve. You can throw down your own father for power! I only demand fealty . . . to me."

T'Challa felt a pull, a surge of energy, and whether it was from his own will or the supernatural power of the Other, he did not know.

He had a decision to make. His father always talked about sacrifice. Sacrifice was something that rulers had to do now and then to keep their people safe. If he could save Miss Rose and the others, he had to do it, even at the cost of his own life. Twenty-one souls for one didn't seem unfair.

"Release them," T'Challa said, gaining control of his thoughts. "Release our friends from the book and I will do as you say."

"No!" Zeke cried out. "You can't do this, T'Challa. It's too dangerous!"

The Other extended a long hand. Flame licked along his fingers. "Take my hand, Young Prince. Take my hand and walk with me. I will let your people go, if that is what you desire. They are nothing to me. The souls this fool Achebe took will be released, and I will deal with him . . . in other ways. Come. Open the book. Turn the page. Seize the power, and you will become a demigod here on earth."

T'Challa hesitated. He wondered for a moment if he should leap and attack the monstrosity in front of him. He clenched his fists. "Do it now," T'Challa said. "Release them."

The Other turned his head toward *The Darkhold* on the cave floor, red mist still swirling around it. He turned both hands palms up and whispered. Flames danced on his palms. T'Challa could not understand the words. They were of a language never before heard on this earth.

Zeke and Sheila wavered on their feet, as if the very words being uttered could send them into despair and torment.

"It is done," the Other said.

"Where are they?" Zeke demanded, coming back to himself. "How do we know we can trust you?"

The Other's flaming eyes landed on Zeke. Zeke trembled and turned away.

Thin streams of what looked like smoke began to pour forth from the closed pages of *The Darkhold*, as if it were on fire. "They will be returned to you as they were," the Other said. "No harm has come to them. Come, Young Prince. We made a pact, you and I."

"No!" Zeke and Sheila shouted at the same time.

T'Challa looked to his friends. "I have to. I made a promise, and I will not break it."

He took a breath and stepped toward the Other.

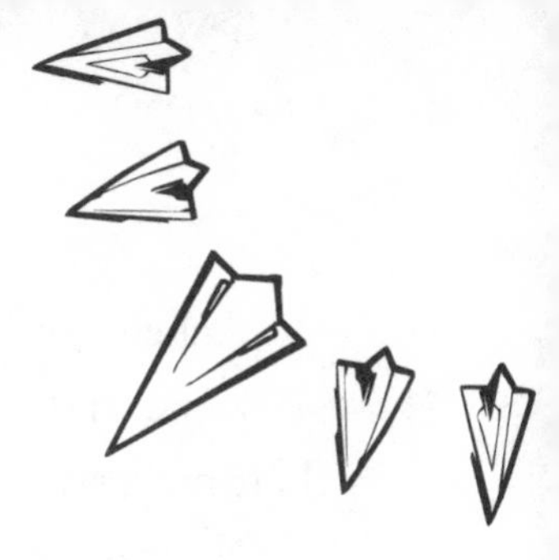

CHAPTER TWENTY-SEVEN

Darkness. All around. A suffocating emptiness that felt like death.

Wind roared in T'Challa's ears, but he didn't see any other sign of its effects. There was only . . . nothingness.

A void.

T'Challa looked up. A glittering canopy of stars winked above him.

Where is this place?

He could not see the ground beneath his feet but took a cautious step and landed softly on firm earth. And then it all came rushing back.

Achebe and his insane puppet.

Zeke and Sheila trying to help and being burned for their bravery.

Nightmare dangling helpless in the air.

Achebe smearing T'Challa's blood on *The Darkhold*.

And, most unsettling, T'Challa offering himself to the Other for the release of his friends and the people of Beaumont.

A sudden gust of wind stirred the air in front of T'Challa. He felt as if he were beyond time and space. *Chthon,* he remembered. *Am I in the realm of Chthon?*

"Yes," a voice spoke. And it seemed to come from nowhere and everywhere at once.

"*The Darkhold* is calling, Young Panther. Are you worthy?"

T'Challa shivered.

"Where are you?" he called. "Who are you?"

"I am What Dwells Beneath," the voice replied.

And that's when T'Challa saw the source of the voice: a man in a ragged cloak who had appeared in the near distance, his face hidden within a deep hood, the only thing visible being two burning embers for eyes.

The figure drew closer. He moved as if a silent wind were propelling him forward. The cloak he wore swept the dark ground beneath him. T'Challa tensed. Even though he wore the Panther suit, a powerful weapon in itself, there was no way he could defeat Chthon. He was beyond death. He was death itself.

“Is it all you truly desire?” Chthon tempted him, now only steps away. “Releasing those pitiful human souls from the pages of my book?”

“Yes,” T’Challa said, avoiding the demon’s gaze. “What do you want? I promised I would come.”

T’Challa couldn’t make out Chthon’s face. There was only emptiness there in that hooded cloak—emptiness and eternal suffering.

“Come,” Chthon, said, raising a hand. It was burnt, T’Challa saw, with dry red cracks, just like Mika’s face when she was possessed. “Look, and behold what may come.”

T’Challa stood still a moment, wondering what was about to happen. A bright light clouded his vision. He waved his hand in front of his face. A myriad of images swam before him, as if he were looking through a kaleidoscope.

He saw himself back in Wakanda, but he was no prince. He was *King* T’Challa now, sitting on the Panther Throne, his subjects bowed down before him. Mounds of jewels, rubies, and gold piled at his feet in offering. The masses shouted his name in praise. “T’Challa! T’Challa! T’Challa!”

He saw himself dressed in ceremonial clothing, the claw necklace around his neck, his private security force, the Dora Milaje, at his side, their spears ready to be unleashed at his command. Wakanda’s secret police, the Hatut Zeraze, were there, too, their faces hard and unforgiving.

He saw nations all over the world tremble at the mention of his name: Black Panther, Emperor of Wakanda.

He saw a great caravan of faithful citizens, walking across a desert of swirling sands only to be near him.

He even saw Zeke and Sheila seated beside him, dressed in traditional Wakandan clothing.

All this was glimpsed in seconds, his destiny. All he had to do was reach out and . . . take it.

"I can give you immortal life," Chthon said as the vision faded. "You will be a king for all eternity. All the power you could ever desire will be at your fingertips, if you only swear to me."

No, T'Challa thought as he struggled against the images in his head. *I don't want this.*

"But you do want it," Chthon said. "We all want power. It is the great equalizer."

T'Challa's head spun with doubt and fear. He had to get back to Sheila and Zeke. How?

T'Challa suddenly felt the sensors in his suit responding to . . . *something.* Small pulses ran along his arms and legs, reacting to another presence nearby. He looked left, then right.

And that's when he saw it.

A darker shade of black loomed behind Chthon. And within that shape two pinpoints of brilliant blue shone. T'Challa's imagination filled in the rest of the shape, although it was shadowy and almost transparent, as if he were seeing a ghost: four strong legs that seemed to be carved from the blackest ebony. A massive head. Jaws that looked as if they could crack a person in half.

And the eyes. Blue beyond blue. A blue deeper than the ocean and brighter than a brilliant sky. Eyes that had seen the first Wakandan walk from the depths of a primordial forest.

Bast.

The Panther Goddess.

Protector of the Panther Clan.

"It can't be," T'Challa whispered aloud.

"Come," Chthon called. "Come, my prince."

I'm not your prince, T'Challa thought.

The demon god outstretched his arm, and it seemed to grow in length, as if it were some kind of serpent, tempting him. It took every ounce of willpower for T'Challa to not close his eyes in fear.

Bast, T'Challa whispered inside his head. *Come to my aid. Free me from this nightmare.*

"Come," the demon god called again.

A stillness settled over the place T'Challa found himself in. Chthon's eyes went from red to green, shifting and changing, a chameleon in demonic form. "Ah," he said, turning his head and sniffing. "Someone . . . some . . . *thing* is here . . . in my domain."

A blue light flared in the dark. T'Challa shaded his eyes against the sheer power of it. And in that light something was revealed. Something that had been there in the darkness all along but only just now seen.

Faces.

Thousands of ghostly faces hovered in the air. He heard their cries and moans, their anguish and despair as they swirled around him. They were everywhere, souls that belonged to Chthon. Trapped here forever.

T'Challa swallowed hard. That would be his fate, too, if he trusted this creature.

Run, Young Panther, T'Challa heard inside his head. *Run.*

The voice was that of a woman, strong and proud.

The voice of Bast.

T'Challa didn't wait. He bolted away as fast as he could, past the hooded figure of Chthon and away from the shrieking souls, into the deeper shades of black that waited ahead.

He ran and ran, not knowing where he was going, his only hope of escape the voice that continued to call out: *Run, Young Panther. Run.*

He heard a roar that shook him to his very core, and then there was darkness.

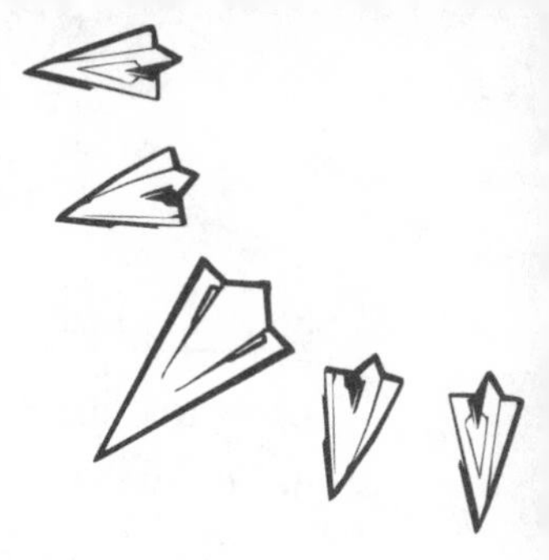

CHAPTER TWENTY-EIGHT

T'Challa felt himself falling.

It was as if he had run to the edge of a great cliff and jumped.

Wind rushed in his ears. Stars and light flashed before his eyes. He was in a black void, a tunnel with no end . . .

He thought he would fall forever, and hoped that this would not be his fate. He still had so much to do. He wanted to see his sister again. And his best friends, Zeke and Sheila. He would be Black Panther one day, King of Wakanda, like his father before him—if he passed the trials. No one ever talked about that. They just assumed that the king's son would inherit the mantle. But T'Challa wanted no favors from his father. He had to prove to himself and others that he was worthy enough to rule the kingdom.

Too many thoughts crowded T'Challa's brain:

The ghostly figure of Bast . . .

Achebe swallowed by *The Darkhold* . . .

And Chthon, a demon god not of this world.

T'Challa closed his eyes.

He saw, as if looking through a rainy curtain, two figures locked in battle. One was a ball of black-and-red flame that shifted into a giant man-shaped creature. Its opponent was a mighty panther, with claws that slashed and ripped.

Is this a dream, or is it really happening? T'Challa wondered. *Is there a place on another plane where the old gods wage battle?*

"T'Challa!" Sheila and Zeke shouted.

T'Challa rolled over. His eyes focused. It was still dark. The flaming light of the Other was gone. He didn't remember hitting solid ground.

"What happened?" Sheila asked.

T'Challa shook his head. He didn't know where he was for a long moment. All he remembered was falling and falling and falling.

"I don't know," he finally said. "I was in this place . . . a terrible place full of darkness." Zeke and Sheila gave him a confused look.

What else was he to tell them? he wondered. That Bast,

the Panther Goddess out of myth and legend, came to save him? That he saw Chthon and Bast locked in battle?

No, he thought. *That story will have to wait for another time.*

Their reunion was interrupted by voices.

T'Challa bolted up.

"What is it?" Zeke asked.

The answer was revealed as several shadowy forms rounded the corner and appeared in front of them.

"Back!" T'Challa shouted, snapping out his claws.

"More creatures of Chthon's," Zeke said. "Here to finish us off!"

"No," Sheila said. "I don't think so."

T'Challa watched in shocked disbelief as the figures of Miss Rose, Mika, Mr. McGuire, and many others appeared before them, their voices a babble of confusion:

"Where are we?"

"What happened?"

"I don't remember how I got here."

Sheila rushed to her grandmother and embraced her.

"Sheila?" Miss Rose said, her eyes wide and still in shock. "Where are we? What happened?"

T'Challa turned to see Mika, who threw her arms around him, catching him off-guard. "What happened?" she asked. "T'Challa? You are here, too?"

T'Challa nodded. He didn't know what else to do. He was still shocked by the physical display of Mika hugging him.

Miss Rose's eyes found T'Challa in the dark. "How did we all get here?" She rubbed her forehead. "I don't understand."

T'Challa tried to form words, but none would come.

"You were kidnapped," Sheila said, addressing the dazed crowd. "But we rescued you. There was a methane leak from the cave. You were all passed out. We found you just in time."

Great thinking, T'Challa thought. *And quick.*

"Yeah," Zeke added. "Um, we were on this cave tour, and, um . . ."

"The important thing is that you're all safe now," Sheila said.

"Right," Zeke put in. "Now we have to get you out of here. C'mon, everybody. Form a line and hold hands!"

Relief flooded T'Challa's body. He rubbed his jaw where Achebe had struck him, and felt one of the claw points on his skin. He paused.

The Panther suit. I'm still wearing it!

He cast a quick glance at Zeke and held up a finger, telling him to wait.

Zeke cocked his head, confused, but then opened his mouth and nodded, as if he understood.

T'Challa quietly slipped away and changed out of his suit. *Is it really over?* he wondered. *Where did I go? Was I really saved by Bast?*

He placed his suit in his bag and threw it over his shoulder.

As they helped everyone out of the cave, Sheila used her phone to call 911. There was a story that had to be told. Beaumont's kidnapped citizens had been found, and T'Challa and his friends had followed clues to rescue them. There was no sign of the evil man who had taken them, but they were safe now, and that was all that mattered.

CHAPTER TWENTY-NINE

"I can't believe it," Zeke said. "We actually had another crazy adventure. How come this only happens when you're here?"

The day after the summer solstice was bright and sunny, and the trio sat outside in Miss Rose's backyard. Two red cardinals flitted and danced in the magnolia trees. The darkness of whatever dimension T'Challa had found himself in was slowly fading.

"That's a good question," Sheila said, narrowing her eyes at T'Challa, a look that was surely just for laughs. "Why do you always bring such drama?"

"I don't know," T'Challa replied.

But he did know.

He was the son of T'Chaka, the Black Panther. Trouble and danger would follow him for the rest of his life.

The screen door squeaked open, and Miss Rose came out holding a tray. "Thought you kids could use some sweet tea," she said. She set down the tray on one of the small tables and wiped her brow with the back of her hand. "Hotter than the devil's breath out here."

T'Challa picked up a glass. Beads of condensation ran down it. Ice cubes tinkled as he raised it to his lips and took a long swallow. "Ah," he exclaimed. "Thank you, Miss Rose. That's just what I needed."

"Mmm-hmm," Miss Rose said. "And what *I need* from my granddaughter is an explanation of what really happened. A police officer came by and took my statement after they talked to y'all, but I don't remember anything. She said everyone else had the same answer—that they woke up in the mines, dazed and confused." She eyed her granddaughter. "I wanna know how you kids ended up in that cave all the way out in Red Mountain. How did I get there? I don't . . ." She closed her eyes and shook her head.

T'Challa saw Sheila swallow nervously. Zeke's expression read as *Don't ask me.*

Sheila set down her glass. All her movements were very deliberate, T'Challa noticed, as if she was giving herself enough time to formulate an answer. *Please have an answer,* he thought.

"Well," Sheila finally said, and, to T'Challa's amazement, actually launched into the truth of what happened. Kind of.

T'Challa held his breath as Sheila told her grandmother that the man who called himself Bob used hypnosis as a weapon; that he wanted to kidnap the citizens of Beaumont and get a ransom from the government; that she and Zeke and T'Challa had discovered his plan when he gave his speech from the internet, using hypnosis and trigger words to get people to respond to his commands. Of course, T'Challa was relieved to see that she didn't mention that they had encountered a flaming demon from another dimension.

T'Challa winced.

He still couldn't come to terms with what had happened in that place beyond time and space. Bast.

The Panther Goddess.

When he was a child and his father told him of his lineage, he said that Bast would answer his call if he ever found himself in grave danger. Every Black Panther throughout Wakandan history had a connection to the Panther Goddess through the heart-shaped herb, the plant that gave strength to those who would rule the kingdom and wear the mantle.

But T'Challa wasn't the Black Panther yet. Maybe it was a message of some sort, he imagined. That one day he *would* rise to the throne.

Miss Rose nodded along through Sheila's explanation but with a healthy air of skepticism. She paused, and her expression changed to one of befuddlement. "I did watch that video, though. It was going around on email. Someone sent it to me. I don't know who. This was right before I was supposed to meet my breakfast bunch." She tilted her head, and her voice grew softer. "I watched it. I remember now. I couldn't turn away. It was like I was being . . ."

"Hypnotized?" Sheila ventured.

"Yes," Miss Rose said. "Like being hypnotized." She paused, coming back to herself. "Well, what happened to this . . . man? Bob? The police said they didn't find him?"

An image of Achebe being overcome by *The Darkhold* flashed through T'Challa's mind.

T'Challa looked to Sheila, who opened her mouth, but seemed to be fumbling for words.

"He must've got away," T'Challa said. "We didn't see him, so he probably discovered our plan to rescue everyone and then escaped."

Miss Rose looked at T'Challa and nodded. She still seemed dazed, to T'Challa's eye.

"I don't know how you kids did all this," she said, "but I think the town owes you a big debt of gratitude."

"Maybe we can get the keys to the city!" Zeke said enthusiastically, and then: "Wait, what do people actually *do* with the key to the city, anyway?"

There was a pause, and T'Challa laughed. Sheila joined in, and finally, Miss Rose had to chuckle as well.

"I still have some questions," T'Challa said.

"Me too," Zeke and Sheila responded at the same time.

The basement was still Base Camp, although the room no longer held the dramatic air of intrigue and discovery. The photos and news articles had been taken off the wall, and it once again looked like an ordinary old basement.

"That word," Zeke said. He paused and lowered his voice. "*Solstitium*. I collapsed when Achebe said it."

"Some type of trigger," Sheila said. "Remember his speech? He said something like 'I will call on you. Wait for my voice,' and then he said it. Solstitium."

Zeke rubbed his forehead, as if Achebe still had control over his thoughts and actions.

"Maybe once you were kidnapped," Sheila said, "he used that word to control you and the others."

"But how did we even get out there?" Zeke asked. "To the cave? I still don't understand."

"Maybe he had help," T'Challa said. "Maybe some of those people in the Vitruvian Man T-shirts drove you out there. They were at the rally, guarding the stage, like bodyguards or something. Remember? Maybe they were hypnotized as well."

Zeke nodded. "I do remember that." He paused and rubbed his hand. "Why didn't Achebe just buy the book from Mr. McGuire? Why did he have to kidnap him?"

"I was wondering that, too," Sheila replied. "But remember what Mika said? She said that the book wasn't for sale.

So if Achebe wanted it, he'd have to steal it and then take Mr. McGuire out of the picture so he couldn't identify him or tell police."

"Sounds right," Zeke said. "I guess."

"And," Sheila went on, "I guess he wanted to offer people's . . . souls . . . to Nightmare as a reward of some sort, so he kidnapped Mr. McGuire."

"Like killing two birds with one stone," T'Challa said, "although I hate that expression."

"How 'bout *feeding* two birds with one *scone*?" Zeke suggested.

"Zeke!" Sheila exclaimed. "Brilliant. You're not so bad after all. I don't care what people say about you."

"Ha-ha," Zeke replied. He rubbed his hand again. T'Challa winced and recalled the moment: his friends trying to grasp the book—*The Darkhold*—and paying for it with a wound they would carry forever.

He took a closer look at Zeke's open hand. A red stripe ran down the center of his palm. "Does it hurt?"

"Not really," Zeke replied. "Itches."

"Mine, too," Sheila added, gently stroking her palm with her other thumb. "I rubbed some salve on it."

T'Challa felt a twinge of . . . he didn't know what. Guilt? Anger?

"I'm sorry it happened," he said. "You were both brave. Braver than a lot of people would have been."

"Well," Zeke said. "You know what we used to say, right?"

"What?" T'Challa asked.

"One for all . . ." Sheila said.

"And all for one," Zeke finished.

T'Challa smiled.

They sat in silence for a while, and T'Challa looked out at the trees and flowering plants. The warm air had cooled off a bit, and the breeze felt good on his face.

He absently turned a bead on his Kimoyo Bracelet. "So Achebe convinced Nightmare to get in our heads and bring us here because he wanted . . ."

"Your soul," Zeke said. "His crazy ritual needed your royal blood, as he called it."

"That and the iron ore," Sheila added.

T'Challa's stomach pitched.

"He said it would be revenge," Sheila pointed out. "Your father, T'Challa. He must have done something to him at one time, maybe before you were born. That's why you didn't know about him."

T'Challa shook his head at the strangeness of all the revelations. He'd have to ask his father or do his own research. He still wasn't sure he would even tell his father what had happened. *But I probably will,* he thought. *It's the right thing to do.*

"That other man," T'Challa started. "Nightmare. I saw

him when we were leaving the arcade. I said I saw a strange-looking man. Remember?"

"Yeah," Zeke said. "I do."

"Surprised Chthon didn't kill him," Sheila said.

T'Challa suddenly felt a twinge of sadness for Achebe. Even after what he had done, or attempted to do. Was he still alive? Consumed in the pages of *The Darkhold*? Trapped in the murky world that Chthon called his home? T'Challa shivered just thinking about it.

But it was over now.

He had done what he had to do to keep people safe.

And that was what the Black Panther was destined to do.

CHAPTER THIRTY

After a dinner of meat loaf, mashed potatoes, green beans, and sweet candied yams, the trio retreated to the backyard. T'Challa patted his stomach. He knew he would have to pay the price soon for all of his . . . overindulgence. He saw his trainer, Themba, once again in his mind's eye.

"Can't say you didn't do anything over the summer, can you?" Zeke offered.

T'Challa grinned. "No. I guess not."

"Don't worry," Sheila said. "He'll be back soon enough."

T'Challa cocked his head. "Sure I will. Someday."

"Well," Sheila said, "I'm sure it'll be sooner rather than later." She gave him a sly smile.

"What are you talking about?" T'Challa asked. He really had no idea what Sheila was getting at.

"To see Mika, of course," Zeke said.

"Mika?" T'Challa echoed.

Sheila sighed. "T'Challa, me and Zeke both saw it. You're smitten."

"Good word choice," Zeke said.

"Smitten?" T'Challa repeated.

"Yeah," Zeke said. "She hugged you in the cave."

"And," Sheila put in, "when you guys were speaking French to each other in the store, you were all moon-eyed."

T'Challa swallowed nervously. He was embarrassed and felt a trickle of sweat run down his forehead. He did like Mika. He just hadn't admitted it to himself yet.

"She did give me her number," T'Challa confessed. "When we left the cave."

Zeke's mouth fell open.

"Ladies' man!" Sheila put in.

"Oh, stop!" T'Challa shouted. "Enough!"

But they didn't, and they teased him for the rest of the night.

The trio tried to fit in as many activities as possible before T'Challa had to head back home. But there was still one thing he had to do.

Downstairs, Zeke and Sheila gathered around. T'Challa tapped a bead on his Kimoyo Bracelet.

"Who are you calling?" Zeke asked breathlessly. "The Black Panther? The real one?"

Sheila chuckled.

The small screen appeared, and the face of a young girl came into view.

"Hey, sis," T'Challa said.

"T'Challa!" Shuri exclaimed.

"Hey," Zeke said, curious. "That's your sister."

"Is that Zeke?" Shuri asked. "Let me see him."

T'Challa flicked his hand over the screen, and it floated to the wall and expanded.

Shuri waved furiously, and Zeke and Sheila returned the gesture.

"I've heard all about you," Shuri said. "Zeke likes to read comics, and Sheila's into science and technology."

"And we've heard a lot about you, too," Sheila replied.

Shuri gave a bright smile and then suddenly became serious. "So. I have some questions for you."

"Me?" Sheila said, surprised.

"Yes," Shuri said. "What do you know about the three laws of thermal dynamics?"

"Oh," Sheila said. "Oh my. Well . . ."

T'Challa looked to Zeke, who shrugged his shoulders.

After a lengthy discussion that went way over Zeke's and T'Challa's heads, T'Challa bid his sister farewell.

"Wait," he said before he hung up. He looked to Zeke and Sheila and then back to his sister.

"Have you ever heard of a man called Bob, the Good Doctor? Or Achebe? He's from Ghudaza."

Shuri scrunched up her face a moment. "Why do you want to know that?"

"Um . . ." T'Challa stammered. "I'll tell you all about it when I get home."

Shuri nodded and reached for something out of frame. A second later, she was cradling a small globe in her palm. She tapped it once, and it began to spin, seemingly of its own accord. "Ghudaza," she said.

A red line traced the outline of the country on the globe, and then, to Zeke's and Sheila's amazement, it lifted away from the globe and hovered in the air. The detail was incredible, and the topography of the country was clear to see—from mountain ranges to rivers and forests.

"Wow," Zeke whispered. "How come you don't have one of those, T'Challa?"

T'Challa looked at Zeke. "I couldn't bring everything, Zeke!"

"Achebe," Shuri said, focusing on the matter at hand. "Wakanda. Ghudaza. Bob, the Good Doctor. Associations and history."

The small hologram of Ghudaza turned into a 3D image.

"The detail search globe has way more functionality than my Kimoyo Bracelet," T'Challa told Zeke and Sheila. "It's linked to the Kimoyo supercomputer network."

They didn't reply. Their mouths were hanging open.

Squares of text began to form around the map, each one full of information.

"Cool, huh?" Shuri said, grinning.

A beep sounded, and one of the squares pulsed with a red outline around it. Shuri read: " 'The Reverend Doctor Michael Ibn al-Hajj Achebe. A civil war broke out in his country and he, along with many other displaced people, sought refuge in' "—Shuri paused—" 'Wakanda.' "

Shuri turned away from the image. She stared at T'Challa. "What are you up to, big brother?"

Zeke and Sheila stiffened, as if caught snooping. T'Challa swallowed.

"I'll tell you about it later," T'Challa replied. "Maybe."

Shuri shot him a curious look, then briefly glanced at Zeke and Sheila. "And . . . it's okay to, um, give you this information? Like, right now?"

"Oh," T'Challa said. "They're okay. Even Father knows about them. Trust me. It's fine."

Shuri grinned. "Wish I could tell some of my international friends about our lives," she said.

"You will," T'Challa said. "Soon enough. So. The map?"

Shuri let out a breath and went back to the map.

" 'Once in Wakanda,' " she continued to read, " 'he tried to overthrow the government, but was stopped by . . .' Dad?"

T'Challa shook his head. "This had to have been years ago."

"I don't remember hearing about it in my studies," Shuri added.

More evidence of my own nation's secrecy, T'Challa mused.

Zeke and Sheila remained silent.

"Well," T'Challa said. "Tell Father I'll be back soon. I'll see you then, sis."

Shuri waved her hand over the map, and it winked out.

"Okay," Shuri replied. "Remember to bring me something? A souvenir? Maybe one of those old dialing telephones. Or wait a minute. What's it called? A boom box! See if you can get your hands on one of those." Zeke and Sheila laughed.

"Okay, Shuri," T'Challa promised her. "I'll try."

"Bye!" Shuri waved. "Nice to finally . . . meet you."

"You too," Zeke and Sheila replied at the same time.

The image on the wall winked out.

Sheila sighed contentedly. "She's cool."

"Yeah," Zeke added. "She looks just like you."

T'Challa's eyebrows knit together. "No, she doesn't."

"Does too," they both replied in unison.

T'Challa screwed up his face. *"Really?"*

CHAPTER THIRTY-ONE

"Never did make it to the Tuscaloosa River for that canoe trip," Sheila said the next day.

T'Challa held his tongue. Fighting raging rapids was the last thing he wanted to do. He was mentally and physically exhausted. The strange conflict they had found themselves in was over, but he still felt a lingering cloud of apprehension, as if Chthon could appear at any time and pull him back into that dark underworld.

"Hey," Zeke said, studying his phone. "Listen to this. There's a summer party tonight at the bowling alley. All kids invited. Food, bowling, and prizes."

"Sounds like a good way to end your trip, T'Challa," Sheila said.

T'Challa agreed. Doing something fun sounded like a good idea.

He only had one question.

What, exactly, was bowling?

T'Challa bowled another strike.

"Unbelievable," Zeke said for the third time.

"You sure you've never played before?" Sheila asked.

"Nope," T'Challa replied. "Guess I'm just a natural."

The bowling alley was full of kids from the surrounding neighborhoods, and the noise was deafening: the thud of bowling balls hitting the wooden lanes, the crash of pins falling, and the shouts and screams of about seventy-five kids.

It was just the distraction T'Challa needed.

Zeke busied himself with eating as many free hot dogs as he could, and now held his stomach and closed his eyes. "Too . . . many . . . wieners," he moaned.

Sheila couldn't help but scold him. "Serves you right."

"Serves you right," Zeke shot back in an accurate mimicking tone.

T'Challa chuckled at their constant back-and-forth.

"Bonjour, T'Challa!"

T'Challa spun around.

Mika's bright smile seemed to light up the room. T'Challa swallowed. "Hi, Mika. How's it going?"

T'Challa did an internal eye roll. *How's it going? What a dumb thing to say.*

"I'm good," Mika replied. "Though I still don't know how I got to that cave. That is, how do you say . . . totally insane?"

"Right," T'Challa replied. "*Totes* insane."

Sheila looked at Zeke and raised an eyebrow. "Did you teach him that?" she whispered.

"Nope," Zeke replied.

Zeke and Sheila watched as T'Challa fumbled his way through a conversation. In English this time, they were glad to hear.

"Wanna try one?" T'Challa asked, handing Mika a ball.

"Sure," she said.

"It's easy," Sheila said. "Just pretend like you're about to smash the patriarchy."

T'Challa's attention was drawn away as a group of kids a few lanes down started shouting. Mika's ball went crashing down the lane, knocking down three pins. She jumped and clapped for herself.

"What's going on down there?" Sheila asked.

T'Challa saw an older man in a security-guard uniform scolding the group of kids. "Y'all too old to be here. Tonight is just for the kids."

One of the boys, who was a foot taller than the security guard, shoved him, sending the man teetering into a cart that held hot dogs and sodas, spilling the mess everywhere. "Back up, old man," he taunted him.

The other boys laughed as the man wiped soda from his pants and shirt.

T'Challa fumed inside. He really disliked bullies. He remembered his first visit to America with his friend M'Baku, where they had encountered several bullies while posing as middle school students in Chicago. One kid named Gemini Jones was particularly troublesome. These guys seemed to be cut from the same cloth. They were mostly all talk and preyed on smaller kids or those who couldn't fight back.

One of the boys snatched the security guard's cap and did a little dance around him while his friends laughed and egged him on.

T'Challa snapped. "That's it," he said, and made his way over.

As he drew closer, the tallest boy noticed his approach and turned to face him. "You looking for something?"

T'Challa didn't answer. "Are you okay, sir?" he asked the man.

"I'm fine, son," he replied. "I can take care of this."

Zeke, Sheila, and Mika were suddenly there, too, taking it all in.

“Don’t worry about them, T’Challa,” Mika said. “Ils sont fous, you know?”

“Yeah,” T’Challa said, “they do seem crazy.”

The tall boy stepped closer to T’Challa. “Who you calling crazy?”

And that’s when the boy swung a long arm.

T’Challa ducked, crouched, and spun on his heel, taking the boy’s legs out from under him.

“Wow!” one of his friends cried as the tall boy crashed to the ground. “You see that, dude?”

The tall boy rose back up. A crowd suddenly gathered, murmuring and pointing. The security guard backed away, speaking into his phone.

“You shouldn’t have done that,” the boy said, and lashed out to swing again.

The swing was so slow, T’Challa actually waited a beat before catching the boy’s arm and pushing him back to fall again.

“We can do this all day if you want,” T’Challa warned him.

The boy gathered himself and then gave T’Challa a stare-down. When T’Challa didn’t respond, the boy walked away, muttering.

The boy’s friends gave T’Challa the once-over as they passed, taking the measure of him. “Thanks, son,” the man said. “You’re not from around here, are you?”

T'Challa shot Zeke and Sheila a grin. "No," he said. "I'm not."

I'm T'Challa, he said in his head. *The Prince of Wakanda. Son of T'Chaka. And one day, I will wear the mantle.*